M
I
K
E

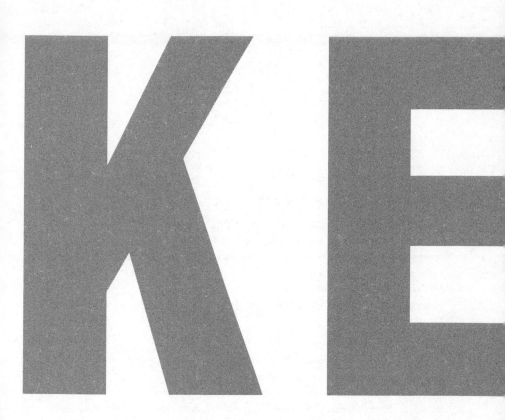

andrew norriss

David Fickling Books

SCHOLASTIC INC. / NEW YORK

All rights reserved. Published by Scholastic Inc., *Publishers since 1920,* by arrangement with David Fickling Books, Oxford, England. SCHOLASTIC and associated logos are trademarks and/or registered trademarks of Scholastic Inc. DAVID FICKLING BOOKS and associated logos are trademarks and/or registered trademarks of David Fickling Books.

First published in the United Kingdom in 2018 by David Fickling Books, 31 Beaumont Street, Oxford OX1 2NP.

www.davidficklingbooks.com

Library of Congress Cataloging-in-Publication Data available
ISBN 978-1-338-28536-9

10 9 8 7 6 5 4 3 2 1   19 20 21 22 23

Printed in the U.S.A.   23
First edition, March 2019
Book design by Maeve Norton

For my lovely friends—
Anna, who first introduced me to Mike,
and Henny, who earns her living
getting people to listen to him.

ONE

This is a true story . . .

Floyd bounced the ball on the ground three times, held it to his racket for a moment, and then threw it into the air in a move he had practiced at least a hundred times a day for the last eight years. His body lifted onto his toes, he swung the racket back up and slammed the ball toward the far side of the court.

As he did so, a movement to his right caught his eye. It was only a momentary distraction, but it meant the ball was a half inch lower in the air when the racket struck and, instead of skimming over the top of the net, it grazed the canvas webbing and deflected fractionally upward before landing back in the court.

"Net!" called the umpire. "First service."

Floyd took a second ball from the clip around his waist and glanced up at the spectators. What he saw didn't entirely surprise him.

It was Mike. Of course.

He was walking along the top row of the tiered seating, his ankle-length black coat billowing behind him in the breeze, and then he turned and began moving down the steps.

Spectators are not supposed to walk around in the stands while a game is in progress. Once a match has started, they stay in their seats and don't move because moving will distract the players. Bouncing the ball a few times, Floyd decided to wait. Presumably, Mike wanted to sit in one of the rows lower down, where he would be closer to the action, and there was no point trying to continue the game until he had settled.

Mike walked all the way down the steps but, to Floyd's surprise, instead of finding himself a seat, he opened the gate in the barrier that surrounded the court and walked over to the umpire's chair.

"When you're ready, Mr. Beresford!" called the umpire.

Clearly, he hadn't noticed Mike, who was now standing a little behind and beneath him.

Floyd pointed with his racket. "You've got a visitor," he said.

The umpire frowned. "Is something wrong, Mr. Beresford?"

"Yes," said Floyd, still pointing at Mike. "Him."

The umpire's frown deepened and he glanced down at Mike before looking back at Floyd. "I . . . I don't quite understand."

"Well, I can't play while he's on the court, can I?" Floyd wondered why the umpire was being so slow. "Could you ask him to leave, please?"

There was a restive murmuring among the spectators, but the umpire made no move to get Mike to leave. His fingers hovered uncertainly over his scoring pad as he looked around.

Floyd's father came onto the court, a look of concern on his face as he walked over to his son. "What is it?" he asked. "What's wrong?"

"Nothing's wrong," said Floyd, "except that I can't play with him there, can I?"

"Who?"

"Him!" Floyd pointed at Mike. "Why does everyone seem to think that someone walking onto the court in the middle of a match doesn't matter?"

Over by the umpire, Mike carefully studied the sky before turning to face Floyd. "Why don't we go for a walk?" he said. "By the sea."

"I am not going for a walk!" Floyd told him firmly. "I am playing tennis. Now, would you please just . . . go away!"

"I didn't say anything about going for a walk," said his father. "And I'll be happy to go away as soon as you tell me what's wrong."

"I wasn't talking to you," said Floyd. A part of his mind was trying to work out why everyone was behaving so strangely. "I was talking to Mike."

"Mike? You mean he's here?" Floyd's father looked sharply around the court. "Where?"

"There!" Floyd pointed. "He's standing right over there!"

His father looked at the umpire's chair and then all around the court. "I'm sorry," he said eventually, "but I can't see anyone."

"But . . . but . . ." Floyd blinked. How could his father not see Mike? He was standing only a few yards away, wasn't he? What did he mean, he couldn't see him? A small tremor of alarm ran through his body as he stared at the figure that, apparently, no one else could see.

"It's all right!" Mike smiled as he raised a hand in a gesture of reassurance. "Nothing to worry about. I'm a friend."

"What is it?" Mrs. Beresford had followed her husband onto the court. "What's happening?"

"He says he can see Mike," said Mr. Beresford in a low voice as he pointed to the umpire's chair. "Over there."

Mrs. Beresford looked in the direction her husband was pointing and frowned. "But there's nobody there!"

"Yes, there is!" Floyd protested. "There's Mike."

"All right, old fellow." Mr. Beresford put an arm around his son's shoulder. "Let's call it a day, shall we?"

"No!" said Floyd. "I don't want to call it a day. I'm playing tennis."

"No, you're not. Not this afternoon. Come along." Mr. Beresford took his son by the arm. "We're going home . . ." And he led his son gently from the court.

It wasn't quite the ending to the tournament that any of them had planned.

Floyd's parents took him to Altringham House, a private hospital on the outskirts of Sheffield that specialized in sports injuries. Floyd had been there before on several occasions, with problems ranging from a torn neck muscle to a chipped ankle bone, and Dr. Willis, who ran the facility, greeted them like old friends. Although it was seven o'clock on a Sunday evening when they arrived, he was waiting for them in reception, and ushered them straight through to his office.

One end of the office was furnished with two enormous leather sofas facing each other on either side of the fireplace, and he motioned Mr. and Mrs. Beresford to one of the sofas, while sitting himself next to Floyd on the other.

"Your father gave me the broad picture on the phone," he said as a nurse brought in a tray of coffee and sandwiches and placed them on the table in front of him, "but you'd better fill me in on the details. What happened exactly?"

Floyd explained how he had been playing in the last match of a three-day Under-18s tournament at Scarborough when Mike had appeared.

"He was winning the thing hands down," put in Mr. Beresford. "He'd won the first set six–two, and he was up five–one in the second and serving for the match."

"So . . ." Dr. Willis turned back to Floyd. "You were all set to chalk up another Beresford victory when . . . the invisible man appeared."

"He wasn't invisible to me," said Floyd.

"No." Dr. Willis helped himself to a sandwich. "How did he do it? Appear, I mean."

"He was just . . . there," said Floyd. "I saw him walking along the top of the stand. Then he came down the steps. I waited, because I thought he was just looking for somewhere to sit down, but he came out onto the court and stood there by the umpire. I couldn't understand why someone didn't tell him to leave. It wasn't till Dad came over that I realized that . . ."

"That no one else could see him." Dr. Willis nodded sympathetically as he finished the sentence. "That must have been quite alarming for you."

"Yes," said Floyd. "It was a bit."

"I take it, from the fact that you knew his name, that you had seen this 'Mike' person before?"

"Yes. Several times." Floyd found himself sweating slightly. Dr. Willis's questions were gently put but made him realize how strange all this must seem to anyone else—indeed, how very strange it all was.

"And when you saw him before . . . what sort of things would he be doing?"

"He'd be watching, mostly. You know. I'd see him standing in the crowd while I was playing, and he'd be . . . watching."

"Had he ever spoken to you before?"

"A couple of times," said Floyd. "But that was when I was practicing on my own."

"And he seemed quite normal?"

"Yes! I never understood *why* he was there, but . . . he always looked perfectly real."

"Hmmm . . ." Dr. Willis sipped thoughtfully at his coffee. "Interesting."

"What do you think it is?" asked Mrs. Beresford nervously.

"Well, that's what we have to find out, isn't it?" Dr. Willis put down his cup. "I think it would be best if Floyd stayed here tonight and we'll run some tests on him tomorrow, but I'll give him a quick check-over now, if that's all right. Make sure there's nothing urgent to attend to." He stood up. "We won't be more than a few minutes."

Dr. Willis took Floyd through a door at the far end of his office that led into a consulting room, where a nurse with a clipboard was already waiting. He gestured to Floyd to take a seat on the examination couch and stood in front of him.

"Just a few questions to start with," he said. "Any headaches recently?"

"No," said Floyd.

"Blurred vision?"

"No."

"Aches and pains in the muscles?" The doctor probed with his fingers at the glands under Floyd's jaw.

"No."

"Any trouble sleeping at night?"

"No."

"Are you taking drugs?"

The question took Floyd rather by surprise. "No," he said. "Never."

"I don't just mean recreational drugs." Dr. Willis looked carefully at Floyd as he spoke. "A lot of athletes know that taking certain chemicals will enhance their performance in some way. Have you been . . . experimenting with anything like that?"

"No," said Floyd. "Absolutely not."

"Sensible fellow!" Dr. Willis smiled and clapped him on the shoulder. "Well, in that case, I suggest we go back and finish those sandwiches, while Janice here sorts out a bed for you."

"Thank you," said Floyd. "Can I ask . . . I mean . . . Is it serious?"

Dr. Willis put an arm on his patient's shoulder as he steered him toward the door. "I think anything that puts you off your tennis is extremely serious, but I don't think you need to worry too much. Whatever the trouble is, we're here to sort it out and we're rather good at that sort of thing! All *you* have to do is make sure you get a decent night's sleep!"

Dr. Willis had the knack of making people believe what he said—it was one of the reasons the Altringham clinic was such a success—and Floyd left the consulting room reassured that, whatever the problem was, Dr. Willis would find the solution and that then . . . everything would be all right.

Floyd's room at the hospital was very comfortable. He had his own television and bathroom, a telephone line to the kitchens in case he wanted anything to eat or drink, and his mother was in a similar room just next door. Mr. Beresford went home—someone had to be there to look after the business on Monday morning—but Mrs. Beresford had promised she would call him as soon as there was any news.

In the morning, a nurse took Floyd and his mother to a different part of the hospital for the first of what turned out to be a long series of tests, scans, X-rays, and exercises on a wide variety of machines. After lunch, he and his mother went for a walk on the grounds, and at two o'clock they went back to Dr. Willis's office, where the doctor sat at his desk and announced that the news was good.

"Physically, you're one of the healthiest individuals I've ever come across," he said, looking at the top page of the open file on his desk. "If I had your fitness recovery times, I'd be a very happy man, I can tell you."

"There's nothing wrong with me?" said Floyd.

"Nothing at all!" said Dr. Willis firmly. "No brain tumors, no trace of drug abuse." He tapped the file with his finger. "Clean as a whistle!"

"If there's nothing wrong with me," said Floyd, "how come I'm seeing someone who isn't there?"

"Yes . . ." Dr. Willis smiled. "Well, now that we've ruled out any physical problem, I think the most likely answer is that we're dealing with a simple mental disturbance, probably brought on by the stresses and strains of your sports career."

"A mental disturbance?" Mrs. Beresford looked at him anxiously.

"No need to be alarmed!" Dr. Willis's smile was as reassuring as always. "You have to remember that our Floyd here is no ordinary racehorse! He's a thoroughbred—a highly exceptional animal—and, as such, exceptional things are bound to happen to him."

"Are they?" asked Mrs. Beresford.

"Your son has been pushing himself to the limit—that's why he's so successful—but that sort of success tends to come at a price." Dr. Willis gestured to the file on his desk. "In physical terms, that price has been the sort of injuries and muscle strains that you won't see on most fifteen-year-olds, and I'm afraid we have to expect the same sort of wear and tear on the mental level, as well."

"Oh . . . ," said Mrs. Beresford.

Dr. Willis leaned forward in his chair. "It's what happens to a lot of top athletes. The mental muscles can get pulled and strained in exactly the same way as the physical ones. But fortunately, when this happens, we have people who know how to treat the damage—in the same way that we have people who know how to treat, say, a sprained ankle."

Mrs. Beresford still looked worried. "You say this happens to a lot of athletes?"

"At some time or another, almost all of the really good ones," Dr. Willis assured her. "Why, only last week I had one of our top marathon runners sitting in that very chair telling me that she couldn't race anymore because her feet had turned to stone. Literally." He gave a chuckle. "But we sorted her out! She'll be running in Vancouver on Sunday." He turned to Floyd. "I'm arranging for you to have a session with our resident psychologist, Dr. Pinner. He's a good man. You'll like him."

"How long will it take?" asked Floyd. "To sort it all out?"

"Well, you can't hurry these things," said Dr. Willis, "any more than you can hurry a torn muscle. You just have to give it the time it needs." He paused. "You're thinking of Roehampton, are you?"

Floyd nodded. The U.K. Under-18s National Tennis Championship took place in Roehampton every June, and this was the year that Floyd was hoping to win the title. He would still only be fifteen, and no one had ever won the national championship at fifteen before, but Floyd's father was convinced that he could do it.

"Roehampton . . ." Dr. Willis consulted the calendar on his desk. "Well, that gives us six weeks, doesn't it? And Dr. Pinner's very good. One of the best. I'm sure he'll have you sorted out by then."

And, because he was Dr. Willis, both Floyd and his mother believed him.

Dr. Pinner was a stocky, broad-shouldered man with a shaved head and the sort of muscles that more usually go with being a rugby player or a nightclub bouncer. But his smile was friendly enough as he welcomed Floyd into his office, and there was a kindliness in his eyes as he cleared a pile of magazines from an armchair and invited Floyd to sit down.

"So," he said, gently removing a cat from his own chair before sitting at his desk and looking across at Floyd, "you're a tennis player."

Floyd nodded.

"And a remarkably good one, by all accounts." Dr. Pinner glanced down at the file in front of him.

"Possibly even good enough to win the national championship—if we can just sort out this business of invisible people wandering onto the court while you're trying to play!" He closed the file and leaned back in his chair. "So . . . any idea who he is, this 'Mike' character?"

"No," said Floyd.

"No ideas at all?"

Floyd gave a little shrug. "Well, I did wonder if perhaps he was a ghost."

"A ghost?" Dr. Pinner looked surprised. "Really?"

"No," said Floyd. "Not really. But I don't see what else he can be."

"Hmm . . ." Dr. Pinner tapped his pen on the desk for a few seconds. "Can you describe him for me?"

"He's tall . . . And he's got this dark, curly hair. And he wears this long black coat over a T-shirt and jeans."

"And how old is he?"

"I'm not sure. A bit older than me, I think."

"And when you look at him, does he remind you of anybody? Anyone you know?"

"No. Well . . ." Floyd hesitated. "The first time I saw him, he did seem sort of familiar. Like I'd seen him somewhere before. Except I hadn't."

Dr. Pinner scribbled something in a notebook. "And when was the first time? Could you tell me about that?"

• • •

The first time Floyd had seen Mike was two weeks after Christmas, in the school gym that Floyd used for his early-morning practice sessions in the winter. Normally, his father would have been with him, but on that particular Wednesday Floyd's mother was in the hospital having a kidney stone removed and Mr. Beresford was doing his best to try to juggle hospital visits, housework, and his business—as well as Floyd's coaching sessions. It meant that, for a week or so, Floyd had to manage the morning practice on his own.

It was while he was setting up the ball gun to deliver some crosscourt shots so that he could work on his backhand that Floyd had realized he was being watched. A glass balcony ran along one end of the room, and when Floyd looked up, he saw Mike staring down at him. He wasn't particularly bothered, but he did think it was odd that someone should be there so early in the morning, and wondered how he had gotten into the building.

The next morning Mike was there again. And the morning after that, while Floyd was gathering up balls to refill the hopper on the gun, he appeared, not on the balcony, but standing by the wall at the far end of the court.

Floyd decided to go over and ask him who he was.

"I'm Mike," said the figure, looking slightly surprised, as if it was something he had expected Floyd to know.

Looking closely, Floyd did have the feeling he had seen him somewhere before.

"Have I played you at tennis or something?" he asked.

"No," said Mike. "I'm not that interested in tennis."

"So why are you here?"

Mike did not answer.

"Because, frankly, I'd prefer it if you went somewhere else," said Floyd. "I'm here to practice, and you hanging around like this is kind of distracting." He turned on his heel and went back to finish loading balls into the hopper. When the machine was ready and he was walking to the other end to continue his practice, he was relieved to notice that, although he had not heard him leave, Mike was gone.

• • •

"You told your parents about all this?" asked Dr. Pinner.

"I did that time," said Floyd.

"And what did they do?"

"Everything." Floyd sighed. "They contacted the police. The headmaster from the school came and talked to me and said if Mike ever turned up again I was to call him directly . . ."

"And did he? Turn up again?"

"No." Floyd shook his head. "Dad came with me to practices after that. Mum was out of the hospital, and Mike never came back. Well . . . not to the gym."

"But . . . ?"

"He started coming to matches. If I was playing in a tournament or a competition, I'd see him sometimes in the crowd, watching."

"And you told your parents about that, as well?"

"Not always," said Floyd. "Mum thought he was a stalker who was going to knife me or something. It made her really . . . upset."

"But you didn't worry about that yourself? That Mike might hurt you?"

"No. No, I didn't." Floyd couldn't say why, but he had never thought of Mike as someone who would harm him in that way.

"Then yesterday," Dr. Pinner continued, "he not only came to watch a match, but walked out onto the court, right?"

"Right."

"And that was the first time you realized that you were the only person who could see him."

"Yes." Floyd looked down at his hands. "I'm not going crazy, am I?"

Dr. Pinner smiled. "I don't think so. You're not the first person this has happened to, you know. There are lots of cases on record. They even made a movie inspired by one of them. Called *Harvey*. With James Stewart. Have you seen it?"

"Who's James Stewart?" asked Floyd.

Dr. Pinner was about to answer when there was a soft beeping sound and he looked down at his watch.

"I'll tell you next time." He stood up. "I'm going to suggest to your mother that she bring you in for three sessions a week starting as soon as possible. Would that be all right with you?"

"Sessions?"

"Yes."

"What does that mean? What do I have to do?"

"You sit in that chair and we talk," said Dr. Pinner.

"That's it?"

"It's usually enough." The psychologist was moving toward the door. "If it isn't, I may have to fall back on the magic green pills, but the talking usually does the trick." Dr. Pinner reached the door but paused before opening it. "I meant to ask. Did he say anything to you?"

"What?"

"Mike. Yesterday. Did he say anything when he walked out onto the court?"

"He suggested we go for a walk," said Floyd. "By the sea."

"Anything else?"

Floyd thought for a moment before answering. "Yes. He said there was no need to worry, because he was a friend."

"Well, that's encouraging, isn't it?" Dr. Pinner was smiling again. "Always good to know you have a friend."

When they got home, Floyd's father was waiting impatiently for details of how the day had gone, and listened carefully as his wife told him about Floyd being an exceptional racehorse, and how nearly all top athletes could expect the occasional mental disturbance. Then Floyd repeated what Dr. Pinner had told him about how seeing people that no one else could see had happened to lots of other people in the past.

"They even made a film about one of them," said Mrs. Beresford. "It was the one with James Stewart talking to a six-foot rabbit, remember?"

"You're not seeing rabbits as well, are you?" asked Mr. Beresford.

"No," said Floyd.

"But the story was based on a real case," said his mother. "Everyone thought James Stewart was crazy, but he wasn't."

"And Dr. Pinner says I'm not crazy," said Floyd. "He reckons if I go to these sessions, we can find out who Mike is and then he'll disappear."

"That'd be good," said Mr. Beresford. "What happens in a 'session,' exactly?"

"We talk," said Floyd.

"You talk? That's all?"

"Dr. Pinner says that's all it usually takes."

"Well, I suppose he's the expert . . ." Mr. Beresford pulled thoughtfully at an ear. "Did he say anything about training?"

"He advised Floyd to go carefully for a bit," said Mrs. Beresford. "He said he should stay in third gear until this has all been sorted out, and not push himself too hard."

"So we have to keep this racehorse in third gear, do we?" Mr. Beresford put a hand on his son's shoulder. "A mixed metaphor like that's not going to be easy!"

"He reckons mostly I can continue as normal," said Floyd. "I can train, do tournaments . . . do whatever I usually do."

"And what happens if Mike turns up again?"

"If he does, Dr. Pinner says I should just treat him like I would anyone else. I can talk to him, or ignore him, or if he gets in the way or something, I can just ask him to move."

Mr. Beresford thought about this. "Maybe we should ease up a bit," he said eventually. "Start a half hour later in the morning, perhaps. And we could scratch the club tournament tomorrow. It's not as if it's important."

Floyd insisted he was fine and there was no need for either of these things, but he did agree to see how he felt the next day before deciding whether or not to play in the tournament, and that he would try starting the morning training half an hour later to see if it made any difference.

"We've been driving you pretty hard for a couple of years now," said his father. "Maybe too hard. Perhaps you need a chance to catch up with yourself."

• • •

After supper, Floyd's parents presented him with a blue-ringed angelfish. It was astonishingly beautiful, with a coppery body and luminous blue lines sweeping up toward its tail.

"But I didn't win," he said. "I only get a fish when I win."

"Your father and I thought," said his mother, "that what you've been through the last couple of days was a lot harder than winning any tennis match. You deserve it."

"We're both very proud of you," said Mr. Beresford. "You know that, don't you? I don't think either of us could have coped with what's happened as calmly as you have."

Floyd took the fish to his room and began the process of transferring it to his aquarium. First, he let the bag float on the surface for a while so that the temperature of the water could adjust to the warmth of the tank, then he tipped the bag on one side and allowed the fish to swim out. He watched as it explored its new surroundings, and came to the decision that he would train tomorrow exactly as normal.

Whatever the doctors at the Altringham clinic might say, he knew that he felt fine. He wasn't stressed or tired and he saw no reason why he shouldn't continue training and playing matches exactly the way he had always. He felt inside himself a fierce determination not to let this thing beat him. He didn't care who Mike was or what he wanted. If he turned up again, Floyd would ignore him and continue what he was doing, regardless. And he would play in the club tournament tomorrow. He would play and he would win, as he was supposed to do, with invisible spectators or without them.

The one thing he was *not* going to do was let someone that only he could see ruin the plans of a lifetime.

"So, how's it going?" asked Dr. Pinner, when Floyd returned to the Altringham clinic two days later for his first session with the psychologist.

"All right, I think," said Floyd. "I'm sort of getting used to the idea, you know?"

"Good, good . . ." Dr. Pinner motioned him to the armchair. "Any more signs of your friend?"

"He turned up yesterday evening," said Floyd. "I was playing in a tournament at the local tennis club, and he was there, watching."

"Did he say anything?"

"No."

"He was just . . . enjoying the tennis?"

Enjoying was not quite the right word, Floyd thought. Mike didn't actually look as if he disliked being there— he had given a little nod and lifted a hand in greeting when Floyd first saw him—but there was no sign that he was enjoying himself. He looked more as if he was *waiting* for something.

"Perhaps," said Dr. Pinner, "the next time you see him, you could ask him to join us for one of these sessions here. Or all of them, if he'd like."

"Join us?" Floyd could not keep the surprise out of his voice. "Why?"

"So we can talk to him," said Dr. Pinner. "Ask him what he wants."

"I don't care what he wants," said Floyd. "I just need him to go away."

"And I think the quickest way to make that happen," said Dr. Pinner, "will be to talk to him. So if you get a chance, please tell him he'd be very welcome—and that he'd be perfectly safe. Nothing anyone says in this room leaves it without your permission. He has my word on that."

Floyd couldn't help thinking how odd it would look if he were to walk up to someone that no one else could see and invite them to a session with his psychologist. It was a bizarre idea, but then so was everything else about Mike, and if Dr. Pinner thought it would help . . .

"OK," he said. "If I see him, I'll ask."

"Right. Though I doubt if you'll actually have to ask him." Dr. Pinner picked up a notepad and pen and lay down on a leather couch so that he was facing Floyd. "He'll probably turn up here whether you want him to or not. Did you win?"

"What?"

"Yesterday. You said you'd played in a tournament. I wondered if you'd won."

The cat jumped up onto the couch, settling itself on Dr. Pinner's stomach.

Floyd had won—easily—but that was only to be expected at a small club like the Sandown. He was too busy to play there very often these days, but occasionally his father suggested he take part in a competition they were holding, and he always enjoyed being back among people who had known him all his life, who still followed his career with a proprietorial interest, and referred to him, proudly, as "our Floyd."

"Yes, I won," he said, and after a lengthy pause added, "you said we have to talk in these sessions, didn't you?"

"That's the general idea." Dr. Pinner stroked the cat's ears and it purred loudly.

"So what do we talk about?"

"Well, I usually let you decide that," said Dr. Pinner, "but if nothing in particular springs to mind, how about you start with the tennis? When did it all begin?"

• • •

Floyd had no real memories of when the tennis had begun, but he had been told that, before he was two years old, his father started teaching him how to hit a sponge ball over a piece of string tied between the dining room table and a chair on the other side of the room, using a racket with half the handle sawn off so that it wasn't too heavy. By the time he was three, they had graduated to the tennis court in the backyard and were using real tennis balls.

There was a tennis court in the backyard because Floyd's parents owned a business building tennis courts—his mother ran the office while his father organized the actual construction—and throughout Floyd's childhood, Mrs. Beresford had always made sure there was time for a little back and forth with Floyd at several points during the day. Then, when Mr. Beresford got home from work, he would take his son down to the court and together they would flick balls at each other over the net, seeing how long they could keep a rally going, seeing if they could do a rally with only backhands, or only forehands, or only volleys.

Floyd had loved it. And he was good at it, as well. Astonishingly good. And his parents watched his progress with delight and considerable pride.

At the age of five, they entered him in his first tournament at Sheffield's Sandown tennis club. The man organizing the tournament laughed when they said they wanted Floyd's name down for the Under-10s competition. The boy was still so small he could barely see over the net, and the man thought there must have been some mistake. Mr. Beresford assured him that there wasn't and pointed out that there was no rule saying you had to be more than five. Only that you had to be under ten.

Floyd's opponent laughed as well when he saw him, but he stopped laughing once the game had begun. Floyd played with an intense seriousness, and a disconcerting ability to put the ball in exactly the place his opponent was least expecting. It was only a little club tournament, but Floyd played three matches that day and won them all.

As a reward, his parents took him to a pet store and told him he could choose anything he wanted. To their surprise, Floyd asked if he could have a fish, and chose a creature of dazzling yellow and blue that the assistant said was a cherub. As he paid for the fish—and the tank and the gravel and the air pump that went with it—his father promised to buy Floyd another fish every time he won a competition, and his mother said in that case they would soon need a bigger tank.

• • •

"Was she right?" asked Dr. Pinner. "About needing a bigger tank?"

"Oh, yes!" Floyd smiled. A picture of his room at home flashed into his mind. There were five tanks now, all much larger than the one his father had bought originally, and all teeming with fish—guppies and loaches, scissortails and bitterlings—the living tracery of ten years of victory on the tennis court.

In any event, Floyd did not have to invite Mike to the next session with the psychologist at Altringham House. He simply turned up, as Dr. Pinner had suggested he might.

Floyd had spent most of that session describing how his tennis career had unfolded so far. He had sat in the armchair and told Dr. Pinner how, when he was seven years old, his father had brought in his first professional coach—old Mr. Palliser—and how these coaching lessons had grown longer and more frequent. First a midweek coaching hour had been added, which took place after school, and then an additional session on the weekend.

By the time he was thirteen, Floyd's schedule had developed into the full-blown routine of a professional athlete.

Each weekday he would be up at six and out on the court by quarter past. In winter, or any time it was too wet, he and his father would drive to an indoor court in the gym loaned by a private school two miles away and do their training there. Floyd practiced his serves, played a few rounds of flash tennis, and then spent the remaining time returning the lobs, backspins, and volleys that his father fired at him from the ball gun.

After two hours, there was just time for a quick shower and some breakfast before bicycling to school. Two days a week there was another two-hour session on the courts after school, along with some weight-training. On Wednesdays there was a session with his new coach, Mr. Ableman, and on the other two days Floyd went swimming because it helped with his fitness and flexibility.

It sounded, Dr. Pinner commented, like a lot of work. Floyd agreed, but it was work that had paid off. At thirteen, he had won his first international tournament in Lisbon. A year later, at the European championship in Stuttgart, he made it through to the quarterfinals, and the following January at the Orange Bowl Championship in Florida—the world championship for Under-18s—he got through to the third round before being knocked out by someone almost five years his senior.

Now the main target in Floyd's sights was the U.K. Junior Championship at Roehampton, and despite his age, he was confident he would win. He would take the Under-18s national title, leave school, turn professional, and then . . .

"And then what?" asked Dr. Pinner, lying on the couch, idly pulling the ears of the cat on his stomach.

"And then . . . well . . . Wimbledon . . . ," said Floyd.

"That's the dream, is it? To play at Wimbledon?"

"Not *play* at Wimbledon," Floyd corrected him. "Win."

"And you think you can do it?"

Floyd had been about to reply that he *knew* he could when he heard the sound of movement. Turning, he saw Mike sitting at the window. His black coat was trailing on the floor, his chin was in his hands, and he was staring intently at Dr. Pinner.

"He's here?" said Dr. Pinner when Floyd told him. He pushed the cat to the floor and sat up. "Where?"

Floyd pointed to the window seat.

"And what's he doing?"

"He's not doing anything. He's just sitting there, looking at you."

"Well . . ." Dr. Pinner stood up and walked over to his desk. "Shall we ask him?"

"Ask him what?"

"Why he's here and what he wants," said Dr. Pinner. "I don't know about you, but I would very much like to know."

Floyd turned to Mike. It felt a little strange to be talking to someone he knew wasn't really there, but the Mike by the window seemed as real and solid as he always had.

"What . . . what do you want?" he asked.

Mike, however, did not answer. Still staring at Dr. Pinner, he gave no indication that he had even heard the question.

"What did he say?" asked Dr. Pinner. He was sitting at his desk, ready to take notes.

"He didn't say anything. He hasn't moved. He's just sitting there, staring at you."

Dr. Pinner nodded. "He's probably trying to decide if he can trust me or not," he said. "So, for the record, I will just repeat that he's safe to say anything he wants in this room. Nothing will ever be repeated outside it without your consent." He paused. "Now . . . can he tell us why he's here?"

Mike seemed to consider this, but then glanced across at Floyd and shook his head.

Floyd felt a brief burst of frustration. "Oh, for goodness' sake, why not?"

But Mike did not respond to that at all.

"No reply?" asked Dr. Pinner.

"No," said Floyd. "I'm not sure he even knows."

"Oh, he knows," said Dr. Pinner thoughtfully. "He's just not ready to tell us yet."

Mike appeared at all of Floyd's sessions with Dr. Pinner after that. Sometimes he would be waiting there when Floyd arrived, more usually he would turn up at some point after the session had started. Not that Floyd ever actually saw him appear. Instead, he would be talking to Dr. Pinner and suddenly realize that Mike was sitting at the window, or lying stretched out on the carpet behind him, or just standing by the bookshelves, his hands thrust deep into the pockets of his long black coat, whistling silently to himself.

But although he was always there, Mike never spoke. At some point in each session Dr. Pinner would suggest repeating the questions about what Mike wanted and why he had appeared, but Floyd's "friend" always refused to be drawn in. He would either turn away, or shake his head, or simply ignore the questions altogether. For nearly a month, he did not utter a single word.

As the weeks passed, Floyd found it increasingly frustrating. Roehampton was getting closer daily and, as far as he could see, the psychologist was making no progress at all. Mike was still there, all too visible—at least to Floyd—and if he was around at the time of the championship, and still liable to walk out onto the court and disrupt a game . . .

The sessions themselves were also a considerable inconvenience. When you included the travel time to and from the clinic, they took up a sizeable chunk of an already busy week. They disrupted training, and the previous week they'd meant that Floyd had had to withdraw from a tournament in Grenoble—his last opportunity, before Roehampton, to play against Barrington Gates.

Barrington, at that time, was receiving his first real attention as the rising star of British tennis. Tall, good-looking, usually to be found with a girl on one arm—or on both—he had recently gotten to the finals of two Under-18 European championships and was, according to Floyd's parents, the only serious rival he would be facing at Roehampton. Whether by chance or design, Floyd had only ever played against him on three occasions, and none of those had been in the last eighteen months. Grenoble would have been the ideal opportunity to see him in action and to look for any unexpected strengths or weaknesses.

But instead of flying out to France, Floyd had stayed in England so that he could sit in a chair and talk to Dr. Pinner. He did not mind sitting in a chair and talking, but he did mind that it didn't seem to be getting him anywhere. Nothing had changed. There was still no resolution to the problem that threatened all of his carefully laid plans and . . . well, in that case, was there really any point in going on?

Then, a little over four weeks after Floyd had started at the clinic, Mike did say one sentence.

• • •

It was a Saturday morning, and Floyd was telling Dr. Pinner about his parents' plan to move to America if, as they hoped, Floyd won the championship at Roehampton. A friend of Floyd's father, Daniel Rowse, ran a tennis school in Florida and had offered Floyd a place there. The weather would mean he could train all year-round and the coaching would be the best in the world, but Floyd was not sure he wanted to go.

Dr. Pinner asked him why.

"I don't know." Floyd found it difficult to put his reasons into words. He just knew there was something about the whole idea that made him . . . uncomfortable.

"Is it the money?" asked Dr. Pinner. "You've spoken several times about how much your parents have spent on your coaching and training . . ."

"I don't think it's that," said Floyd. "Dad's always said the money's not a problem."

"I suppose it would mean saying good-bye to all the people you know in England," said Dr. Pinner. "Is that something that bothers you?"

But it wasn't really that either. Playing tennis as much as he did, Floyd had never had time to make the sort of friends who would keep him from moving to a different country.

"Perhaps it's your parents you'd miss," suggested Dr. Pinner. "That would be understandable. You are very close to them."

"No, no." Floyd shook his head. "They'd come with me."

"Both of them?" Dr. Pinner looked surprised. "But who's going to look after the business?"

"They'll sell it," said Floyd. "It's what they always planned and, once I go pro, I'll need someone to manage travel arrangements, hotels, equipment, sponsorship, press releases, and so on. Mum and Dad'll do all that."

"I see," said Dr. Pinner. "Have you told them you're not entirely happy about all this?"

And Floyd was about to reply when Mike interrupted.

"Tell him about Mr. Crocker," he said.

"What?" Floyd was rather startled.

"Your parents," said Dr. Pinner, "I was wondering if you'd discussed . . ."

"No, I was talking to Mike," explained Floyd. "He says I should tell you about Mr. Crocker."

"Does he, now?" Dr. Pinner reached for his notes. "You'll have to remind me. Who was Mr. Crocker?"

"He was my first tennis coach."

"I thought your first coach was a man called Palliser." Dr. Pinner was riffling through the pages of his notebook. "The old guy with the glasses who taught you how to do a drop shot. You've never said anything about a Mr. Crocker."

"No," said Floyd. "I forgot."

And it was true. Until Mike had said the name, Floyd had completely forgotten about Mr. Crocker.

When Floyd was six, his father told him that it was time he had a coach. Someone properly qualified, who could help him develop his game. They were particularly lucky, Mr. Beresford said, that the official coach for their county was none other than Gerald Crocker, a man who had trained three of the U.K. champions of the last twenty years. Normally, he only worked with children over the age of ten but he had agreed to make an exception in Floyd's case after seeing him at the Sandown. So, once a week, every Thursday after school, Floyd was taken to the county tennis courts in Sheffield for a lesson with three other children.

Mr. Crocker might have known a great deal about tennis and about coaching, but Floyd found him rather frightening. He was a big man, with a booming voice that echoed around the windy tennis courts when he shouted, and he seemed to spend a good deal of his time shouting.

Some days, Mr. Crocker didn't just shout. When his students were slow to grasp what he was explaining or failed to do the shot he wanted them to practice, he would express his irritation with a quick smack of his hand on the back of their heads. Although he never used his full strength, it could still be painful.

He never hit Floyd, or Caroline, who was the only girl in the group, but if either of the older boys started playing up or fluffed a shot that Mr. Crocker thought they should have returned with ease, the voice would roar out and the burly figure would come striding across the court, and the hand would smack on the back of a head as he told them what they had done wrong.

Floyd tried to remind himself it was a privilege to be taught by the man who had trained three British champions. But however much he reminded himself, he did not enjoy going to the tennis coaching on a Thursday and on three occasions made up an excuse not to go. The first time he said he had a stomachache, the next time that he had an aching wrist—his father was always careful to ensure that he didn't overstrain his young muscles—and on the third occasion he claimed that he had a headache. This time, however, his father ignored the excuse, drove him to the courts, and left him with Mr. Crocker, who, it soon became clear, was in a particularly impatient mood.

He was angry with the ball gun that didn't seem to be working properly. He was angry with one of the older boys who had forgotten to bring a spare racket, and he was angry with Caroline, who was complaining of the cold and wanted to be allowed to wear her sweat suit. She seemed to be mistiming every one of her practice serves even though he had explained to her very forcefully how important it was to relax. When she missed a simple volley in the game that followed, he came striding across the court toward her, bellowing in frustration, and actually had a hand raised to give her one of his little clips on the back of her head.

Caroline flinched, but the blow never landed because at that moment Mr. Crocker realized he was being watched. There was someone standing on the path that ran along the back of the courts, and Mr. Crocker changed the movement of his hand to a cheery wave of greeting.

Floyd turned around and saw his father, a deep frown on his face, staring across at them from behind the wire mesh.

"Hello, there, Peter!" Mr. Crocker boomed cheerfully. "You decided to stay and watch?"

Mr. Beresford did not reply, but opened the gate in the side of the wire mesh that surrounded the court and walked over to his son. Completely ignoring Mr. Crocker, he looked down at Floyd.

"You look cold," he said. "Let's go home."

Floyd walked over to the side to pick up his bag and sweater. Behind him, he could hear Mr. Crocker, his voice no longer booming, but sounding uncharacteristically apologetic.

"Look, Peter, I hope you didn't get the wrong impression. You know I wouldn't do anything to hurt them. They just need a little prod occasionally, that's all."

His father did not reply. He did not even look at Mr. Crocker but stood there, waiting in the middle of the court, until Floyd had collected his things. Then, without a word or a glance at the coach, he took Floyd's hand and walked him back to the car.

On the way home, they stopped off at an Italian restaurant for some garlic bread and melted cheese, which was Floyd's favorite food, and then followed it with some ice cream.

They didn't talk about tennis until, as they were leaving, Mr. Beresford said, "I think in the future we'll skip the lessons with Mr. Crocker. Go back to just you and me, playing at home. Is that all right?"

Floyd agreed that, yes, that would be all right.

"The most important thing about tennis," said his father as they walked toward the car, "is that it's supposed to be fun. That's when any of us do our best at something. When we're having fun." He looked down at his son. "I want you to promise me something."

"What?" asked Floyd.

"I want you to promise me that the day tennis stops being fun, you'll tell me and we'll stop doing it, OK?"

• • •

Sitting in the office with Dr. Pinner, Floyd found that for some reason the palms of his hands were damp with sweat, and he wiped them on the side of his trousers.

"He's a good man, your dad." Dr. Pinner was lying on the couch, staring up at the ceiling. "I can see why you admire him so much."

"He's brilliant," said Floyd. "I'd do anything for him."

"Yes," said Dr. Pinner. "I'm beginning to realize that."

10

The next day, when Floyd was playing in a simple single-elimination tournament in Bournemouth, Mike made an appearance on court during a game. It was the first time he had appeared anywhere outside Dr. Pinner's office since Floyd's sessions with the psychologist had started, and in an almost exact repeat of the incident at Scarborough, Mike walked out onto the court and stood beneath the umpire's chair, with a vague look of dissatisfaction on his face.

Floyd knew better than to complain and ask for him to be taken away this time. He simply ignored him and continued with the game, which he won, but it left him feeling, as he told Dr. Pinner on the following Monday, both annoyed and frustrated. There were, he reminded the psychologist, less than two weeks until the championship at Roehampton and, despite the fact that they had been meeting three times a week for over a month, they were still no nearer to finding out what was going on. Or getting rid of Mike. Or finding out why he had appeared in the first place.

What was particularly annoying, Floyd thought, as he made his complaint, was that Mike himself was sitting cross-legged on the floor beside him, nodding sagely in agreement.

"Did you tell your parents about it?" asked Dr. Pinner when Floyd had finished describing the incident.

"About Mike?" said Floyd. "No."

"Why not?"

"I didn't want to worry them. I mean, there's nothing they can do, is there?"

"Maybe not." Dr. Pinner was sitting at his desk, twirling a pen between his fingers. "But tell me . . . if you'd strained a muscle in this tournament, would you have told your parents about that?"

"Yes, obviously, but . . ."

"So you'd tell your parents about something like a strained muscle—even though there's probably nothing they could do, except make sure you rested—but you don't tell them when someone only you can see walks onto the court while you're playing. I wonder why."

There was something in the psychologist's tone of voice that Floyd found distinctly irritating.

"I told you. I didn't want them to worry."

"You're sure that's all it was?"

"Of course I'm sure! What else would it be?" Floyd's annoyance was reflected in his voice. "Look, I've been coming here for over four weeks now, and as far as I can see all this sitting around and talking isn't getting me anywhere. Mike's still here, he's still distracting me at tournaments, I still have no idea who he is, or what he's doing—"

"You don't know who he is?" Dr. Pinner interrupted. "Really?"

"No, of course I don't!" Floyd looked at the psychologist suspiciously. "Do you?"

"Well . . ." Dr. Pinner gave a little shrug. "It's not *that* difficult to work out, is it?"

"Yes, it is!" said Floyd. "At least, it is for me. I'm not a psychologist, remember? I'm a tennis player." He paused. "So who is he?"

"It's best if you work these things out for yourself," said Dr. Pinner, "but I can give you a couple of clues, if you like." He thought for a moment before continuing. "We're talking about someone that only you can see, that only you know exists, and whose name . . . is Mike." He paused again. "Does that help?"

"No," said Floyd. "It doesn't."

"OK," said Dr. Pinner. "Second clue. What's *your* name? Your full name."

"Floyd Michael Beresford," said Floyd, and it took a second for the penny to drop.

"Me? You think he's me?"

"Well, I don't see how he could be anyone else really, do you?" said Dr. Pinner. "He's not *all* of you, obviously. But a part." He looked curiously at Floyd. "You really didn't know?"

"In psychology," said Dr. Pinner, "we call it projection. It's when a part of the mind is projected out onto something or someone in the outside world. I'm sure you've come across this idea in books, or heard about it in school?"

"No," said Floyd. "Never."

"Well, perhaps I can give you an example . . ." Dr. Pinner drummed his fingers on the desk for a moment before continuing. "Let's suppose that there's a part of you that wants something *really* badly, but you can't come out and *say* that's what you want, because it would be too dangerous. In fact, the whole idea is so dangerous, you can't even allow yourself to *think* it, so as a defense your mind decides to hide the idea somewhere else. One way it can do that is by 'projecting' it onto another person."

"What sort of dangerous idea?" asked Floyd.

"Well, one example might be that you were gay, and you lived—"

"I'm not gay," said Floyd.

"But if you were," said Dr. Pinner, "and you lived in a society that put people in prison or even killed them for being gay, you would have very strong reasons for denying those feelings in yourself. Simply to survive, you might need to push them away, to hide them. And, as I said, one way to hide them is to project them onto someone else. That way, you get to pretend they're not your feelings at all and you can disapprove of them like everyone else does."

Floyd stared at him blankly.

"Sometimes, however," the psychologist continued, "there isn't anyone suitable for you to project the feelings onto. There's no one around who can represent this 'dangerous' idea and, in those cases, the mind can sometimes actually invent somebody—a completely imaginary person—and make *them* responsible for whatever it is they don't dare think themselves. Small children do it all the time. Instead of admitting they knocked over the milk or broke the plate, they'll say their imaginary friend did it."

"You think Mike is an imaginary friend?"

"A sort of grown-up version of that, yes."

Floyd glanced across at Mike, who was standing at the window, looking out at something in the gardens and showing no interest whatever in the talk going on behind him.

"And you think he's a part of me that wants to do something dangerous?"

"Yes."

"Something so dangerous that I have to pretend it's his idea and not mine?"

"Yes."

"So what is it? What is this idea that's so dangerous?"

Dr. Pinner made a little gesture with his hands. "That's what we're trying to find out, isn't it?"

Floyd stared at him. "You already know, don't you?"

"What I know, or think I know, isn't important," said Dr. Pinner. "These things only have real meaning if you discover them for yourself."

"And how am I supposed to do that?"

"Well, if you think about it"—the psychologist smiled encouragingly—"Mike's already told you. More or less."

"Mike hasn't told me anything," protested Floyd. "We keep asking him what he's doing here and he never answers."

"According to my notes"—Dr. Pinner tapped at his notepad—"Mike has spoken to you on three occasions so

far, and I'd argue that he told you something very important each time."

"Oh, come on!" Floyd felt a sudden surge of anger without quite knowing why. "All he's ever said was that I
should tell you about a tennis coach I had when I was six,
and invited me to go for a walk by the sea!"

"And I think he had a very clear message for you on
both those occasions," said Dr. Pinner, "but possibly not
as clear as the *first* thing he said to you. That's when he
really laid it out."

Floyd tried to recall what it was that Mike had said to
him on the first occasion, but for some reason it was difficult to remember when the first occasion had been, let
alone what Mike had said. In the last few seconds, his
vision had narrowed, and there was a sort of fog in his
brain that made it difficult to focus . . .

"It was when you were practicing on your own in the
indoor courts at the school," said Dr. Pinner. "You asked
Mike who he was, and he told you his name."

Yes . . . Floyd remembered now . . . Sort of . . . Though
what had happened after that was still hazy. The fog in his
head was making it difficult to remember anything . . .

"Then you asked if you'd ever played against him in a
match somewhere," Dr. Pinner prompted.

Yes . . . And what was it Mike had said in reply . . . ?
Something about not being that interested in tennis . . . ?

But what was so special about Mike saying that...? Except that... hadn't Dr. Pinner said Mike was a part of himself...? And if Mike had said he wasn't that interested in tennis, that would mean... That would mean...

It was, Floyd later said, as if someone had pulled the pin on a grenade inside his head. For a brief moment he was no longer in Dr. Pinner's room on the first floor of the Altringham clinic, but somewhere indefinable where he was looking at... his whole life. Not just a part of it. All of it. All at the same time, in a single moment that seemed outside of time altogether.

He saw himself with his father playing to-and-fro across a net in the dining room, and laughing. He saw his mother taking him down to the tennis court in the backyard and encouraging his first attempts to get the ball over the net and how proud she had been when he succeeded. He watched all the hours he had spent with his parents learning to make the ball go where he wanted it to, and how much fun it had been.

But, in the same timeless moment, he was also watching himself as the practice and the training grew more serious. He could see the part of his mind that began to wonder, as he endlessly practiced his serve... *Why am I doing this?* He was practicing his backhand against endless shots from the ball gun and asking himself... *What was the point?* And he was playing in tournament after tournament, making such huge efforts to win, while all the time thinking . . . *What did it matter? Winning or losing. What did any of it really matter?*

Because the truth was . . . he was not that interested in tennis . . .

He was not that interested in tennis.

And then he was back in Dr. Pinner's office and the sweat was running down his face, and he was gripping the arms of the chair as if desperate to keep his balance.

Dr. Pinner was no longer behind his desk, but sitting on a chair directly in front of Floyd, an expression of kindly concern on his face.

"Deep breaths," he was saying. "That's right . . . deep breaths . . . you're fine . . . well done . . ." He patted Floyd's arm. "Very well done! Here." He held out a glass of water. "Have a sip of this."

As Floyd took the glass, he turned to the window where Mike was still standing. He was no longer staring out at the gardens below but had turned and was looking at Floyd, with the sort of smile on his face that you might give a companion when, after a hard day's climbing, you had both finally made it to the top of a mountain together.

And then he vanished.

"He's gone," said Floyd.

"You mean Mike?" Dr. Pinner was over at the sink, pouring another glass of water for himself.

"Yes."

For some reason, Floyd found, Mike's disappearance had left him overwhelmingly sad. As if he had actually lost a real friend.

"Well, I suppose he's done what he came to do." The psychologist returned to his chair in front of Floyd. "How are you feeling?"

"Terrible."

The psychologist smiled sympathetically. "Yes, I can imagine . . ."

There was, of course, another thought even more painful than losing an invisible friend.

"If my parents find out about this, it'll kill them!"

"That might be a slight exaggeration . . ."

"No, it's not!" said Floyd. "My tennis is what they live for! Everything they do is for that. They've spent years working for it. It's the only thing they've ever wanted!"

"Yes . . ." Dr. Pinner put his head on one side. "Why is that, do you think?"

"What?"

"Well, it's not every parent who decides to train their son as a tennis star from the age of two, is it? Why *did* they have that particular dream, do you think?"

It was not something that Floyd had ever considered before, possibly because the answer seemed so obvious.

"Tennis is their life. It always has been. The tennis club was where they met, where they got married, where Dad turned pro and . . ."

"Yes, your mother told me about that." Dr. Pinner had stood up and was carrying his chair back to behind his desk. "She said that considering his background and how late he started, getting as high as he did in the rankings was an astonishing achievement."

"Seventh," said Floyd. "He was ranked seventh in the U.K. And he'd have been number one without the accident."

"Ah, yes . . . the accident . . ." Dr. Pinner nodded slowly. "Athens, wasn't it?"

Athens was indeed where the accident had happened, only a year after Floyd's parents got married. His father was there for a tournament. He had played and won his first round and was heading back to the hotel when he was knocked down by a drunk driver. The surgeons did a remarkable job on the shattered bones of his right leg, and these days he walked with only a slight limp, but the dream he had had of a career playing professional tennis had been shattered in a way that could never be repaired.

"Your mother told me it's the only time in his life that she's seen your dad give up," said Dr. Pinner. "His whole future had been snatched away from him, and for a while he thought there was no point going on, until . . ."

She saved me. That was what his father had said, remembered Floyd, on the one occasion he had talked to him about it. *Your mother saved me.*

"Because she came up with a new dream, didn't she? Your dad might never be a champion himself, but by then she was expecting a baby, and she suggested maybe their child could have the chance to achieve all the things that his father had been denied.

"That was the new dream, and it wasn't a bad one. But it was *their* dream, not yours. Which didn't matter so much when you were a child, but now you're growing older, and what you do with your life is something you'll need to decide for yourself. It'd be wonderful for everybody if what you wanted to do was play tennis, but . . . that *isn't* what you want, is it?"

Floyd could not deny it. He knew the truth now. He did not want to spend the next fifteen years on a tennis court. Nor even the next fifteen weeks.

There was a long period of silence when neither of them spoke, and the more Floyd thought about it, the more impossible it all seemed. He had come here to get better, he thought, and all that had happened was that he felt worse.

Much, much worse.

Dr. Pinner advised Floyd, in the short term at least, to keep the discovery he had made to himself.

"I think you've had quite enough excitement for one day," he said as Floyd was leaving. "You need to give yourself time to process it all. Let it soak in for a bit. Next session, we'll start talking about what you want to do, and how best to tell your parents."

Floyd agreed. Telling his parents that he was "not that interested in tennis" was a conversation he was happy to postpone for as long as possible. What he wanted most at the moment was somewhere quiet, where he could lie down and go to sleep.

When his mother drove Floyd home that evening, however, he found his father had other ideas. Mr. Beresford met them in the hallway, sounding particularly excited and cheerful.

"It's a celebration!" he said. "In fact, a double celebration! You've both got ten minutes to get changed. I'm taking us all out to dinner."

A quarter of an hour later, at a table in the corner of the Italian restaurant that had seen them celebrate innumerable triumphs over the years, Mr. Beresford explained that the first cause of celebration was that he had found a buyer for their company. He had put out word the week before that he would shortly be selling his tennis court construction business, and someone from the Sandown club had already expressed a keen interest.

"It means," he said happily, "that when you go to Florida, we can all go together, like we planned! The timing's perfect!"

But the even better news, he went on, was that the seedings for Roehampton were in and Floyd had been placed second. Barrington Gates was the number one seed, as they had always known he would be, but the organizers had decided that Floyd, still only fifteen, was ranked just behind him.

"He's going to get the shock of his life when he plays you this time," said Floyd's father with a chuckle. "He's not going to know what hit him!"

"I've got some film of him you ought to watch," said his mother. "He's good, but I think he's lazy. If he's made to move around the court too much, he gets flustered."

They discussed tactics for a good part of the evening, and if Floyd was quieter than usual, his parents did not seem to notice—though in fairness, there was a good deal going on to distract them. Several of the other diners in the restaurant—which had always been popular with members of the Sandown tennis club—took the opportunity to come over and congratulate Floyd on being second seed and to wish him well at Roehampton. Then, while they were waiting for dessert, Mr. Tullio, the restaurant manager, appeared with a cake lit with a dozen sparklers and *Good Luck!* written in icing on the top, along with a card signed by everyone on the staff.

It was only toward the end of the evening, when Mrs. Beresford had gone to the restroom, that Floyd's father inquired, almost casually, how things had gone that day with Dr. Pinner.

"I don't mean to pry," he said—he knew that what went on in Floyd's sessions with the psychologist was private—"but it has been several weeks now and . . . I mean, is he getting anywhere? Is he . . . sorting things out?"

"I think so," said Floyd.

"Good . . ." His father hesitated for a moment. "But he still turns up occasionally, does he?"

"You mean Mike?"

"Yes."

Floyd wondered briefly how best to reply, and decided he could tell at least part of the truth.

"Well," he said, "I'm not sure, but I think he's gone."

"Gone? You mean gone for good?"

"I think so. Yes."

"Oh, that is excellent!" Mr. Beresford clapped his hands in delight. "You know, I had a feeling when I got up this morning that it was going to be a good day, and it's just kept on getting better and better!" He beamed across at his son. "Did you ever find out who he was?"

"Mike?"

"Yes."

"Dr. Pinner reckoned that he was a projection."

"A projection? What's that?"

"It means he was an outward expression of some inner . . . anxieties," said Floyd. "About tennis and stuff."

"Oh, yes?" His father was nodding again. "And how do you know?"

"What?"

"That he's gone."

"Dr. Pinner says that's how it works. Mike was a projection of these unconscious feelings and anxieties, so when I made them conscious, there was no need for him anymore. And he's gone."

"For good?"

"That's what Dr. Pinner thinks."

"Wonderful! Absolutely wonderful!" Mr. Beresford turned to his wife, who had just gotten back from the restroom. "He's gone!"

"Who has?"

"Floyd's friend, Mike! And Dr. Pinner reckons he's gone for good!"

"Really?" Mrs. Beresford looked at Floyd.

Floyd nodded.

"Oh, that is such a relief!" Mrs. Beresford reached out and took her son's hand in her own. "I don't mind telling you we've been *very* worried." She sat down. "Did you find out who he was?"

"Turns out he was a projection," said Mr. Beresford.

"What's a projection?" asked Mrs. Beresford.

"I'll explain it to you later," said her husband. "The point is, he's gone, and Floyd's got a clear run to

Roehampton." He was grinning from ear to ear. "Oh, that is such wonderful news!"

And it was there in the restaurant, with his parents smiling across at him, and with the pride and happiness shining from their faces, that Floyd understood what he was going to have to do.

14

"I wanted to ask," said Floyd, at the start of his next session with Dr. Pinner, "if there's anything you can do about it."

"About what?"

"About the part of me that doesn't want to play tennis," said Floyd. "The part that isn't . . . interested. I wondered if there's anything you can do about that."

"You mean can I help you make those feelings go away?"

"Yes."

"No," said Dr. Pinner. "I'm afraid not."

"I only ask," said Floyd, "because at the first session we had, you said that if all else failed you could try the magic green pills and . . ."

"That was a joke," said Dr. Pinner. "I'm sorry, but there aren't any magic pills. Not ones that'll let you play tennis, anyway."

"I thought not," said Floyd, "but I wanted to check. And you're quite sure there's nothing *I* can do?"

"Not that I know of, no." Dr. Pinner was sitting with his feet up on the couch, his hands clasped behind his head, his legs stretched out in front of him, the cat asleep in his lap. "We want what we want, I'm afraid. We can deny it sometimes, but we can't change it."

He looked across at Floyd.

"I know how disappointing all this must be. You came here to sort out Mike so you could go back to playing tennis, and I promised I'd help you do that and ... and I really thought I could."

He let out a long sigh, and then sat up, pushing the cat to one side and swinging his feet down onto the ground before continuing.

"You know why people come to me, Floyd? Ninety-nine times out of a hundred, the people who wind up in this room are here because they're frightened. It doesn't matter what the sport is or how successful they are, that's almost always what causes the problem. There's a part of them got frightened. Frightened of winning. Frightened of losing. Frightened they're not good enough ...

"And I can do something about that. I can talk to the part of them that's scared and teach it *not* to be frightened. I can give them exercises that'll boost their confidence and sharpen their focus and help them relax at times of stress . . ." He pointed a finger at Floyd. "But the part of you that doesn't want to play tennis isn't frightened. It just doesn't want to play tennis."

Neither of them spoke for a while.

"I've been thinking about what to tell my parents," said Floyd.

"Oh, yes?"

"And I've decided I'm not going to tell them anything."

"Ah . . . ," said Dr. Pinner.

"That's what I've come here to say, really. I've decided I'm going to continue playing tennis. There's no way I'm going to tell my parents they've wasted the last ten years of their lives. So I'm going to continue with the tennis, just like they planned."

Dr. Pinner took a deep breath. "Are you going to tell them anything about . . . ?"

"No," said Floyd flatly. "And I don't want you to tell them either. You won't, will you?"

Dr. Pinner gave a little shrug. "Whatever we say in here stays in here, you know that. But I think it's a mistake."

"Yes. I know you want me to tell them—"

"What I *want*," Dr. Pinner interrupted, "has nothing to do with it. I just don't think it'll *work*. You might get away with it in some fields, but . . . this is top-line sport we're talking about. If you want to succeed, it has to be all of you, every single part of you, and if you don't have that . . ."

"It doesn't matter," said Floyd. "If it turns out I'm not good enough, that's OK. Dad'll be disappointed, but I'll have tried. I'll have done everything I could."

"Have you considered," said Dr. Pinner, "that although you're not very interested in tennis, there might be something else that you *do* want to do?"

"I know there is."

"You do?"

"Yes," said Floyd. "I want to make my parents' dream come true."

• • •

When Floyd told his parents that he would not be returning for any further sessions with the psychologist, they were at first delighted. They were less sure after they had received calls from both Dr. Pinner and Dr. Willis at the Altringham clinic urging their belief in the importance of Floyd continuing his treatment.

In the end, though, they went along with Floyd's decision. As Mrs. Beresford said, they didn't really have much choice. Floyd had clearly made up his mind, and short of physically dragging him to the clinic, there wasn't a great deal they could do about it. But they could, she suggested, keep a careful eye out for any signs of anxiety and strain, and make sure he wasn't overdoing it. As the days passed, they watched and were relieved to see no sign that this might be the case. If anything, their son seemed to be training with even more energy and determination than usual, and Mr. Beresford actually found himself urging his son to slow down.

Floyd, however, was reluctant to slow down for any reason. Slowing down gave him time to think, and those were the times when unwelcome thoughts crept into his mind. Thoughts like what a relief it would be to do as Dr. Pinner had suggested and admit to his parents that playing tennis for up to six hours a day was not what he really wanted . . .

Keeping busy was the best means of holding such thoughts at bay, though they still leaked into his life at unsuspecting moments. As he endlessly practiced hitting a ball to make it go where he wanted, a part of his mind would start wondering, *What's the point of it all?* As his father called across to say that it was important to watch his position on the court, Floyd would find himself wondering, *Why? Why would someone call that* important? And in the matches his father arranged for him with opponents down at the Sandown club, Floyd could see in the faces of the people watching how much his winning seemed to matter to them, and he would wonder why winning no longer mattered to him.

But then his mother would appear at the supper table excitedly clutching the details of their hotel booking for Roehampton, or his father would watch him catch a volley and send it, beautifully disguised, to the far corner of the court, and the delight on their faces would remind him why he was doing it all.

Not that it was easy. Keeping the secret of how he really felt did seem to take a lot of energy. More, if he was honest, than he had expected. Though it was only when they got to Roehampton that things got really difficult.

Because at Roehampton, Mike came back.

The U.K. Under-18s National Championships are held each year at the Roehampton tennis club, a few miles north of Richmond in Surrey. In those days the tournament lasted a week, and there were thirty-two entrants, all of whom had earned their place in the competition either by appearing in heats held a few months earlier or by points they had earned in tournaments during the previous year. Then, as now, they are the top young players in British tennis, and the competition is closely watched by anyone who has an interest in the game and wants to see what talent is climbing the ladder.

For Floyd, the trouble began in the first round. His opponent was someone he had beaten on at least a dozen previous occasions, and his parents were expecting an easy victory. He won the first set 6–1, but when Floyd was about to serve at the start of the second set, he looked up to see Mike striding onto the court.

This time, instead of merely standing by the umpire's chair, he began pacing restlessly up and down the side-lines with the same look of dissatisfaction on his face that he had had at Bournemouth.

Floyd's first emotion was of shock rather than annoyance. Hadn't Dr. Pinner said that Mike was a projection of unconscious feelings Floyd had not been able to admit that he had? But he *had* admitted them now, so how could Mike be standing in front of him? It shouldn't be possible.

Possible or not, however, Mike was definitely there, and as the match progressed he did more than simply pace up and down the side of the court. On three occasions he actually walked across in front of the net during a rally. Floyd determinedly ignored him, but the effort took its toll. He won the match, but only after the second set had gone to a tiebreaker.

In the next round, Floyd's match went the full three sets. This time, Mike not only appeared on the court and walked across it while he was playing, but actually stopped in front of the net and stayed there for most of the match, never looking directly at Floyd, but still with that slight wrinkling of the nose at what he saw around him.

It is not easy to serve a tennis ball through the body of someone standing directly in your line of sight, even if you know they're not really there. For the first time in the competition, Floyd lost a set, and only won the third—and the match—with considerable difficulty. As he walked back to the locker room, his father asked if everything was all right.

"You seemed to be having a bit of a problem concentrating out there," he said. "Is everything OK?"

Floyd assured him that it was, but the concentration required to deal with what felt like two opponents on the court instead of one was taking its toll. Floyd wasn't sure how long he could continue doing it.

In the quarterfinals he was due to play Paul Cutter, a seventeen-year-old who looked more like a weight lifter than a tennis player.

"Don't let his shape fool you," his mother had warned. "He's deceptively fast and volleys like a maniac. Try not to let him get close to the net, and play to his backhand—that's his weakest stroke."

Only a part of Floyd's mind was listening to this advice. A larger part was wondering what mayhem Mike might be planning, and he didn't have to wait long to find out. Two games into the first set, Mike appeared on the court and, as Floyd prepared to serve, came and stood directly beside him, close enough for Floyd to hear his breathing and a quiet sigh.

Floyd let the ball drop, bounced it a couple of times on the ground, and wondered what to do. Part of him yearned to shout at Mike to go away, but in front of several hundred spectators that didn't feel like a real option. He decided the only thing to do was try to *imagine* Mike wasn't there, and serve anyway . . .

He tossed the ball in the air with his left hand and was in the process of lifting his right arm for the serve when . . . he found it wouldn't move. Looking down, he saw that Mike was holding his right forearm in a grip that made any movement impossible. Floyd tried to pull himself free, but Mike was stronger than he was. Far stronger. The grip on his arm looked almost effortless, but Floyd's attempts to pull himself away had no effect whatever. There was no way he could break free. No way at all.

"Mr. Beresford?" called the umpire. "Is everything all right?"

And the worst thing, as Floyd later told Dr. Pinner, the very worst thing about it was the look on Mike's face as all this was happening. As they struggled, he could see there was nothing aggressive or malicious in Mike's expression. Quite the reverse. Looking into his eyes, all Floyd could see was an immense kindness, as if Mike thought he was doing a favor for a friend. And as Floyd struggled vainly to get free, Mike actually leaned forward and said, "Don't worry. I won't let go!"

"Mr. Beresford?" repeated the umpire.

Floyd's father appeared on the court, running over with the medical kit in a bag slung over his shoulder.

"What is it?" he asked quietly. "What's wrong?"

"It's my arm," said Floyd. "I . . . I can't move my arm."

"Let's have a look . . ." Mr. Beresford put down his bag and ran his fingers gently down Floyd's arm.

Mike, for some reason, was no longer visible, but Floyd could still feel the grip above his wrist.

"Well, you've certainly done something." Mr. Beresford gently massaged the muscles beneath his fingers. "It feels like they've gone into spasm . . ."

"I'm sorry . . . ," said Floyd.

"Not your fault!" His father smiled. "These things happen."

"I tried, I really tried . . ."

"Of course you did." Mr. Beresford patted his arm. "Don't worry about it. But you won't be playing anymore today, I'm afraid. Come on!" He bent down to pick up the racket that had fallen to the ground. "We'd better tell the umpire."

If his father was disappointed at how the tournament had ended—and Floyd knew how desperately disappointed he must be—he did not show it.

When the umpire announced that Mr. Beresford would be retiring from the competition because of an injury to his arm, a murmur of sympathy ran around the spectators, and there was a generous round of applause as both players left the court.

"What happened?" asked Paul as they made their way back to the clubhouse.

"It's my arm. Seized up. Cramp, I think."

"Well, I hope you sort it out." Paul spoke gruffly, but with sympathy. "I doubt I'll get off so easy next time we meet."

Down in the locker room, Floyd sat on a bench and felt the iron grip on his arm slowly fade. Cautiously, he flexed his fingers and hand.

"Better now?" asked his father, who had appeared with some hot towels and Floyd's kit bag.

"I think so."

"Keep it relaxed and don't move it too much," said Mr. Beresford. "We'll put these on to keep it warm. I'm going to have a word with the officials in case there's a chance of rescheduling, and your mother's organizing a physical therapy appointment for tonight."

Floyd hesitated. "I'm not sure it's a massage I need," he said slowly. "I think I might have to go back to Dr. Pinner."

"Ah." Mr. Beresford sat down on the bench beside him. "I did wonder."

"It was Mike," said Floyd. "He was holding my arm. That's why I couldn't move."

"OK . . ." Mr. Beresford patted his shoulder. "Don't worry. We'll sort this out, I promise you. I don't care what it takes. This time, we'll sort it out."

Floyd wasn't sure what it took to persuade a psychologist to drive down to London from the north of England at the end of a day's work to talk to a fifteen-year-old with an imaginary friend, but by eight o'clock that evening the burly figure of Dr. Pinner was standing in the hotel foyer, in his slightly crumpled suit with patches of cat hair on his trousers.

He said he wanted to speak to Floyd first on his own, and in a private room provided by the hotel manager, he listened carefully as Floyd explained what had happened over the last few days.

"I don't understand why he's back," said Floyd, when he had finished. "I mean, you said he was a projection of ideas I was too frightened to let into my own mind. But I *have* let them in now, so why is he still here?"

"I would very much like to know the answer to that myself," said Dr. Pinner, "but the first thing we have to deal with is that he seems determined that you shouldn't play any more tennis."

Floyd's shoulders sagged. "I know. What am I going to do?"

"I think you have to tell your parents the truth," said Dr. Pinner. "I don't see that you have any choice now. Keeping it a secret is no longer an option, is it?"

Reluctantly, Floyd agreed.

"As I said before, I'm very happy to do the talking if you think that would help. Explain to them what's happened and why."

"Will that stop them from getting upset?"

"No," said Dr. Pinner. "I'm afraid nothing's going to stop them from being extremely upset. At first, they probably won't even believe it. Then they'll get angry with me, and then angry with you . . ." He gave Floyd an encouraging smile. "But eventually they'll get past that. They're good people. They'll just need time to get used to it all."

When Dr. Pinner invited Floyd's parents to join them, Floyd sat in silence as the psychologist explained about projection, about how they had discovered in the sessions at the clinic that Floyd didn't really want to play tennis, how Floyd's reluctance to accept this truth had made that part of him come out as a figure that only he could see, and how it was now necessary that they all accept the truth of his real feelings.

The psychologist described how parents, with the best of intentions, could sometimes project their own desires onto their offspring. He said that while wanting success for your child was obviously not in itself a bad thing, if the time came that the child in question wanted something different, it was important not to force them onto a path they had not chosen for themselves.

Floyd's parents listened with increasingly baffled and bemused expressions on their faces, and he could see that his father, particularly, found the whole story difficult, if not impossible, to believe.

"You're trying to tell us Floyd doesn't want to play tennis?" he demanded when the psychologist had finished.

"Yes," said Dr. Pinner. "It's been extremely difficult for him to accept that, but . . . yes."

"No!" Mr. Beresford banged the table with the palm of his hand. "That is ridiculous! Have you ever *seen* him play? Have you ever watched him out on court? He . . . he was *born* to play tennis!"

"I don't think he was," said Dr. Pinner. "I think he was *taught* to play tennis. And taught, if I may say so, extremely well."

Mr. Beresford gave a derisive laugh. "You think someone gets to be that good just because he's been well taught? Never! Floyd plays like that because he loves the game! He always has. He couldn't play that well if he didn't!"

"I don't think Floyd plays tennis that well because he loves the game," said Dr. Pinner. "I think he plays tennis that well because he loves you. Both of you."

"So it's *our* fault now, is it?" Mr. Beresford's voice was rising with his frustration and his anger. "You think we *made* him play tennis every day? And go to training and coaching and fly to tournaments instead of being out with friends?" He leaned across the table. "Let me tell you, I have *never* forced Floyd to do anything! Never. And you sit there and tell me he doesn't want to play anymore? I don't believe you! And I'm certainly not going to let you talk him out of a career that could make him one of the biggest names in the sport." He turned to Floyd. "You don't think any of this is true, do you? You don't believe him! Surely, you can't!"

It wasn't easy to answer, but Floyd managed one short sentence.

"Yes," he said, "I do."

His father blinked. "Well, I don't! Maybe you're a bit run-down. Maybe we've pushed you too hard and you need a proper rest, but . . ."

"No." Floyd wasn't sure where the voice came from, but he found himself speaking with a decisiveness that surprised him as well as his parents. "I'm not run-down, Dad. I just don't want to spend my life on a tennis court. I wish I did—you can't imagine how much I wish I did—but I don't."

"How . . . how can you say that?" His father was staring at him, openmouthed. "You love tennis! Why would you want to give it up?"

Floyd did not know how to answer that until, from nowhere, the picture came into his mind of the two of them walking across the parking lot of an Italian restaurant when he was six years old.

"Because . . . because it's not fun anymore," he said.

Mr. Beresford stared at him. The blood had drained from his face and he said nothing for several long seconds as he looked across at his son. Then he suddenly stood up and, still without saying a word, abruptly turned and left the room.

"How could you?" It was Floyd's mother who broke the silence, and Floyd saw there were tears in her eyes. "After all he's done for you, how could you turn around and say that to him? All your life, he's tried to make sure you had all the chances he never had himself . . . and now, just when all the years of effort might actually be paying off, you tell him you don't want it anymore?"

Floyd mumbled something about being sorry, but his mother was not listening. With the tears streaming down her face, she stood up and left the room to find her husband.

Dr. Pinner took a deep breath.

"Like I told you," he said, "it's going to take them a while to get used to this one."

● ● ●

Later, up in his room, Floyd sat on his bed and decided that it had been, without question, the worst day of his life. If he could have gone to his parents' room and told them it was all a mistake, and that he had changed his mind, and that he was going to continue playing tennis, he would have done it in an instant.

But he couldn't do that. Because, as Dr. Pinner had pointed out, whatever Floyd said, Mike was not going to let him play tennis. If he tried, Mike would be there to make sure it was impossible. Dr. Pinner had suggested that this might even be the reason Mike was still around. To guarantee that any such attempt would fail.

He and Floyd had spent an hour in the private room downstairs discussing all the possible options, while Floyd wondered desperately if there was an answer that would not cause his parents so much pain. But there wasn't. Sometimes, the psychologist had told him, the only way forward was through the pain, not around it.

For Floyd, it did not feel as if he was on the way forward to anywhere. It felt, instead, as if everything he had ever known and trusted and believed in and loved had been taken away from him, and he had been dropped in a large black hole. Every part of him hurt and that night, before the sleeping pill that Dr. Pinner had provided finally took effect, his mind continued to search for some way out, for anything that would make the situation even slightly better. But there wasn't anything.

There was only the pain.

When Floyd came down to the dining room for breakfast the next morning, he was surprised to find Dr. Pinner sitting at the same table as his parents, and the three of them deep in conversation.

The psychologist was the first to see him and beckoned him over.

"Your parents and I have been talking," he said, "and your father has come up with an interesting suggestion."

"Has he?" Floyd pulled out a chair and sat down.

"Your mother and I have agreed," said his father, "that if you don't want to play tennis anymore, then . . . then that's your choice, and we'll have to live with it. But we want to be quite sure that this really *is* what you want and you're not throwing away an opportunity because you're tired or frightened."

Floyd opened his mouth to speak but Dr. Pinner made a slight movement with his hand to indicate that this might not be the time, and he closed it again.

"You came to Roehampton to play in the championship," Mr. Beresford continued, "and we think that's what you should do. You've entered. We've paid the fees, and we think you should finish what you've started. If, at the end of it, you still decide that you don't want to play competitive tennis, then we'll accept that decision. But we think you should play out the championship." He looked directly at Floyd. "Will you do that?"

"I don't see how I can," said Floyd. "I've already been knocked out of the competition, haven't I?"

"As it happens," said his father, "you haven't. Paul Cutter went out to celebrate last night and broke his ankle jumping off a fire escape, so he can't play in the next round. The officials called me this morning, and they are prepared to let you through. They want to see a semifinal with four players, and since you only lost to Paul because of a cramp . . ."

"It wasn't a cramp," said Floyd. "It was Mike, and if he decides—"

"Yes, we know it was Mike," his mother interrupted, "but Dr. Pinner has an idea about that."

Everyone turned to the psychologist.

"My idea," said Dr. Pinner, "is that you ask Mike if it's all right for you to continue playing in the tournament."

Floyd stared at the psychologist. "You want me to ask his permission?"

"I think it's a reasonable request under the circumstances. As your father said, he and your mother have invested a great deal of time and money in getting you here, and they would like to see you play the thing out. If Mike appears on court this afternoon, I suggest you ask if he's prepared to let you do that. You tell him that if, when it's all over, he still wants you to give up tennis, then, OK, that's what you'll do. But you ask him if you can at least finish what you've started."

Floyd tried to imagine himself out on the court, asking someone only he could see for permission to play.

"Will you do it?" asked his father.

"Yes. Yes, of course I will," said Floyd. He would have agreed to almost anything if it meant not seeing the look of disappointment on his parents' faces again. He looked at the psychologist. "And you think he'll say yes?"

"Let's ask him and see, shall we?" said Dr. Pinner.

• • •

Dr. Pinner, in the conversation he had with Floyd before leaving after breakfast to drive back to the clinic, said that he thought an actual request might not be necessary.

"Mike is, after all, a part of you," he had said, "not a separate person. So anything you know and think, he already knows as well. When you get out on court, it'll soon be clear whether he's up for it or not, but I hope he is. Finishing the tournament would help your parents through what we both know is going to be a difficult time."

The psychologist was right. When he walked out that afternoon to start his warm-up, almost the first person Floyd saw was Mike sitting on the grass bank near the far end of the court, and there was, as Dr. Pinner said, no need for an actual conversation. Mike gave a little wave of acknowledgment, yawned heavily, lay back on the grass, and appeared to fall asleep. Floyd understood that it meant the only opponent he would have to face that day was the one standing on the other side of the net with a tennis racket.

His name was Johnny Cope, a Scot with an impressive serve but little else for Floyd to worry about. Floyd had played against him on several occasions and beaten him each time, though on this occasion it took the full three sets, one of which went to a tiebreak. Floyd was not sure if it was lack of sleep, the trauma of the previous twenty-four hours, or the constant effort needed to fight the increasing reluctance he felt even to pick up a racket—but in a way he did not care. He was doing what he had promised, and now he just wanted the whole thing to be over.

When he shook hands with Johnny over the net, he glanced across at the grass where Mike had slept through the last hour and a quarter, but found he had disappeared.

The final was to be played the next day and it was not a match that Floyd was looking forward to. He would be playing Barrington Gates, and Barrington was in a different league from Floyd's previous opponents. Not only was he an excellent player, he carried a self-assurance on court that had unnerved many an opponent before a match even started. He played with a flair and an arrogance that said he knew he was better than any of his opponents. And he usually was.

The press had recently noticed this as well. In the past month there had been a spate of newspaper articles about how Barrington was the rising star of the tennis world and how, in a few years, British tennis might even have someone capable of winning at Wimbledon. A few weeks before, Floyd had looked forward to the prospect of playing him, but not now.

In his present state, Floyd knew, there was little chance of beating Barrington and, sitting in the locker room waiting for the call to go out on court, he wondered why he was making himself do this. He remembered Dr. Pinner, in his room at the clinic, explaining how in top-flight sports it had to be *all* of you out there on the field to have any chance of winning—and Floyd did not have that anymore. There was a part of him that would instead be dozing comfortably on the grass in the shade. It was marginally better than someone walking in front of the net in the middle of a game, or holding on to his arm so that he couldn't serve, but in the end it didn't make much difference. Either way, he was going to lose, and lose badly.

Behind him, he heard the noise of someone coming into the room. It was Barrington Gates with a friend, and although the match was due to start in less than ten minutes, he seemed in no particular hurry to get changed. This was, Floyd knew, part of a technique designed to unsettle his opponent. Barrington would often turn up at the last minute, apparently unconcerned, and giving the impression he didn't much care about the result because, to him, the match wasn't that important.

His friend was asking Barrington how long he thought it would take to win the coming match, apparently unaware that Floyd, sitting on the other side of some lockers, was in the room and could hear every word. There was a birthday party on a boat, the friend was saying, that they could probably get to if the match didn't go on for too long.

"I can't see it taking more than an hour," Barrington answered. "It's only the kid from Sheffield, isn't it?"

"There's the prize-giving afterward, don't forget," said his friend. "And then you'll have to talk to the press."

"You're right," Barrington agreed. "Better make it an hour and a half. Tell her we'll be there by four."

There was something in the casual arrogance of all this that stirred a deep anger in Floyd. He was not someone who became angry often, but at that moment all the bitterness and frustration and disappointment of the last few days seemed to become focused into a single burst of fury directed at one person. Barrington Gates. He might no longer want a career in tennis, Floyd thought, but that didn't make it any easier to take snubs and put-downs like that. He was filled with a burning desire to wipe the arrogant smile from Barrington's face and make him—

"Me too," said a quiet voice.

Floyd turned and found Mike sitting on the bench beside him. Somehow, he wasn't entirely surprised.

"It's not really to do with the tennis." Floyd found himself speaking quietly as well. "I just want to see him lose."

Mike nodded his agreement.

"And not just lose," Floyd continued, "but lose really *badly*, you know?" An idea was forming in his mind. "I don't suppose . . . I mean . . . Is there any way . . . ?"

Mike smiled. "Be good to go out on a high, wouldn't it?"

"Yes. Yes it would. You think we could do it?"

"Him against us together?" Mike's smile became even broader. "He won't stand a chance!"

"Good . . ." Floyd stood up, suddenly feeling a lot better. "OK, then. Let's show Mr. Gates what it's like to play against a kid from Sheffield!"

• • •

The Roehampton final always drew a sizable crowd, and on this occasion, almost all of them were expecting Barrington Gates to win. He, after all, was the one who had recently received all the media attention, and a large section of the spectators stand was taken up with a group of young girls carrying a banner with WE LOVE BARRINGTON written on it. There was a great cheer when he came out on court, his hair carefully tousled, his sweater hung loosely over his shoulders, waving graciously at his fans. But from the first ball to the last, there was never any doubt about who was going to win.

Barrington won the toss and served for the opening game with a neatly placed ball down the center line, which was returned with such speed and force that he barely had time to make a lunge in its direction—and miss.

Despite the advantage of having the serve, he lost the opening game without winning a single point and then lost the game that followed without returning a single ball. Floyd served four aces in a row. Every one of them landed in a different section of the court, within inches of the line and so fast that Barrington was still trying to take in where it was going when it had already gone.

The crowd watched, at first, in stunned silence. This was not what they had expected. In the third game, Barrington rallied a little, and even took it to deuce before losing to a crushing volley to the edge of the court that brought a gasp of appreciation from the crowd.

Word spread around the grounds of what was happening and more spectators joined the already crowded stands. Old men drifted out from the clubhouse to see what all the fuss was about. Other players abandoned their games on the other courts to come and watch. Even those who knew little about the game could not help but realize they were watching something truly exceptional.

Though in truth it was not so much a tennis match as an execution. After the shock of losing those three opening games, Barrington did his best to retrieve the situation. He was a player with a long experience of battling back from the brink and had a considerable armory of tactics to employ.

He tried to break up the smooth flow of Floyd's game with lobs that drove him back from the net. He tried to wear his opponent down with shots from the baseline that would make him run from side to side and tire him out. He tried taking a defensive posture with long rallies and even resorted to the psychological tricks that players sometimes use to break their opponent's concentration, like asking for the balls to be changed, or "accidentally" losing his racket, or stopping to retie his shoelaces.

Nothing worked. Wherever he put the ball, Floyd would be there waiting for it and the return would be a masterstroke of accuracy and cunning. It would arrive with a speed that made it impossible to return, or a disguised spin that had Barrington completely baffled. And as the match wore on, there was something else. There was something in the ruthless, unruffled confidence of Floyd's playing that was . . . unnerving. Something in the way his face never altered and his expression never changed. It told you he didn't just *think* he could win. He *knew* it.

Barrington was not playing badly, in fact he was playing at the height of his ability, but he was simply outclassed and, long before the match was over, he had come to realize it himself. He had been defeated in his head, as Mr. Beresford would have put it. Floyd wasn't just playing Barrington at tennis, he was killing him, and Barrington no longer believed there was anything he could do about it.

The spectators had come to the same conclusion. From watching in stunned silence, they began to applaud what was clearly an astonishing display from a fifteen-year-old that many of them had never heard of before. The surgical precision with which he placed a half volley within an inch of the baseline to win the fourth game drew the first round of spontaneous applause. After that, it gathered pace. The voices of the Barrington fans cheering their hero grew quieter, while the cheers of delight and astonishment at the skill with which Floyd demolished his increasingly desperate opponent gained in strength with every shot.

Barrington lost the match 6–0, 6–0. He had not won a single game and, in the last two games, as with the first, did not win a single point. As he stepped up to the net to shake hands, he was white and shaking. He looked as if he was trying not to cry . . .

Floyd shook hands without smiling, then glanced at his watch. "You were right," he said quietly. "All over in much less than an hour. Plenty of time for you to get to your party." And he strode off to where the judges were lining up to give him his trophy.

• • •

Standing on the dais, holding the silver cup above his head, with the cameras flashing on all sides of him, Floyd felt no elation, but was aware of a quiet sense of satisfaction. He might not want a career in tennis anymore, but it felt a lot better to finish as the youngest ever U.K. Under-18 Champion than as someone who retired after getting knocked out in the third round. Much better.

It didn't change anything, of course, though his parents were not convinced of that yet.

"I knew it!" his father cried, his eyes alight with pleasure, before uttering a fierce whoop of delight as he stood beside his son. "I knew you could do it! We've got a news conference set up so that you can . . ."

"No," said Floyd, and he was surprised at how calmly he could say what had to be said. "No news conference. No interviews. There's no point."

"You're not still talking about giving up, are you?" His father took his arm. "Because I won't believe it. I won't!"

"I promised you I'd finish this tournament, and I have," said Floyd firmly. "But that's it. Sorry."

"Floyd! Please!" His father was still clutching his arm. "You *won* out there! Don't you realize what that means? You can do anything now! And don't tell me you don't like tennis, because I won't believe you. Not after seeing you play like that."

"I played like that," said Floyd, "because I was angry. I can't spend the rest of my life being angry. I'm sorry. But that was it. That was my last game."

PART

TWO

1

Floyd presumed that, after Roehampton, he had seen the last of Mike. Now that his "friend" had done what he had come to do and any dream of a tennis career had been abandoned, he would, Floyd thought, have no further reason for any of his strange appearances.

It was Dr. Pinner who warned him that this might not be the case, and he put his warning in a letter that he sent a few days after the match with Barrington. His father brought it up to Floyd in his room, where he was cleaning out a fish tank.

"Dr. Pinner's written to you," he said, holding up an envelope. "He wrote to your mother and me as well and said we could read the one to you if we wanted. So we did."

He gave Floyd the envelope, which had not been sealed, and then stood in the doorway while Floyd took out a single typewritten sheet and read what it said.

The psychologist began by congratulating Floyd on winning the championship. He said that, although he had been unable to watch the match himself, he had heard graphic accounts of it from several sources, and one day he hoped very much to hear the full story of how such a victory had been possible.

But it was in the second paragraph that Dr. Pinner explained the real reason he was writing.

You may not want to hear this, but I think I should warn you that I doubt very much that this is the end of your friend's story. If Mike was, as I at first believed, a simple projection of a repressed wish, he would have disappeared when that wish was brought to light. The fact that he reappeared seems to indicate that he is something more and I think, at some point, he will be back.

I hope if that happens that it will not worry you unduly. It has always seemed to me that Mike is, as he said himself, your friend—and a friend with only your best interests at heart. However, if he does return and you think it might help to talk about it, please do not hesitate to contact me. I have told your parents I would be more than happy to discuss things with you, either as a psychologist or as a friend.

In the last part of the letter, Dr. Pinner went on to say how sorry he was that things had turned out so differently from the way everyone had hoped. He said he knew things would be a bit awkward at home for a while, but that he felt sure that Floyd and his parents would work it out, adding that he much admired the way they had all coped with such a difficult and unexpected situation so far.

At the end, he repeated his offer to be available to talk at any time, and gave two phone numbers and an email address where he could be contacted.

"And has he?"

Floyd's father was still standing in the doorway.

"What?"

"Your 'friend,' Mike. Has he reappeared? Since Roehampton?"

"No. No, he hasn't."

Floyd's father sniffed briefly. "So do you want to talk to him?"

"To Mike?"

"To Dr. Pinner."

Floyd considered this. There was a part of him that wanted very much to know why the psychologist thought Mike might return and what it was that Mike might want if he did, but there was another part of him that didn't want to think about any of that. Not now, anyway. What Floyd wanted now was a chance to rest. A few days at least of peace and quiet.

"No," he said. "No, I don't."

"Well, that's a relief." His father turned away. "I'm not sure I could cope with any more help from Dr. Pinner at the moment."

The psychologist was certainly right about things at home being awkward, thought Floyd as his father strode off toward the stairs, but that was no more than he had expected. For as long as he could remember, his family's daily routine had revolved, in one form or another, almost entirely around tennis. Tennis was what they did together first thing in the morning, what they talked about at meal-times, and the future they had planned for in the evenings. It had been the glue that had bound them together as a family, and now . . . all that was gone. The pieces had come unstuck and Floyd could not see any way of ever putting them back together.

Although it was awkward, however, it was not quite as bad as Floyd had feared, and the main reason for this was the way he had won at Roehampton. In the week following the championship, letters and cards of congratulation poured in. They came from family and friends, from other players, from the media and from dozens of commercial companies. There were phone calls from people who had watched Floyd play and now wanted to offer sponsorships for his future career. There were calls from sports reporters and magazines asking for interviews, and there were invitations from tennis tournaments around the world offering Floyd free accommodations and a generous allowance if he would agree to come and play.

It was, Floyd knew, deeply frustrating to his parents that he refused to accept or even reply to any of these offers, but there was also a certain pride in the scale of his achievement. If you have devoted more than ten years of your life to turning your son into a tennis star, it is comforting to see that you achieved at least part of your ambition. It was, as Mike had said, good to go out on a high.

There was another reason that his parents did not seem to be quite as upset as Floyd had expected, and it was that neither of them really believed that he had given up tennis for good. Since winning the championship at Roehampton, Floyd had not so much as set foot on a tennis court, but both his parents were convinced that he would return to the game one day. After much discussion, they had come to the conclusion that they had been pushing their son too fast and too hard. *If we give him time*, Mr. Beresford told his wife, *if we just step back and give him space, he'll come back to it. I know he will*. Given a sufficient period of rest and recovery, they were sure that their son would eventually return to the game in which he displayed such obvious skill.

It was probably with this in mind that at lunch on the same day that the letter from Dr. Pinner arrived, Floyd's father suggested that it might be a good time to take a vacation.

"A vacation?" said Floyd. "Where would we go?"

"*We* can't go anywhere," said his mother. "Not this time of year. You know that."

In the business of building tennis courts, July and August are among the busiest months for orders and construction.

"But we thought you might like to go to Cornwall," said his father, "and stay with your grandmother."

Floyd's grandmother lived in Bude, on the North Cornish coast, and was always asking if her only grandson could come and stay.

"We thought it might be good if you got away from things for a bit," said his mother.

And Floyd thought getting away from tennis and parents and all talk of invisible friends sounded like an excellent idea.

Granny Plum—her real name was Victoria—was waiting on the platform when Floyd got off the train at Exeter.

"Goodness, look at the size of you!" she said, reaching up to give him a hug. "I'm not sure you'll fit in the car!"

She led the way to her little Nissan Micra, but in fact she was the one who had some difficulty squeezing herself in behind the steering wheel, pulling out the seat belt to almost its maximum length before strapping herself in.

"So, how long can you stay?" she asked.

"I'm not sure," said Floyd. "A few weeks? If that's all right?"

"The longer the better as far as I'm concerned!" His grandmother patted his knee as she launched them into traffic. "I've been trying to get your parents to let you come for a real stay for years."

Later, speeding down the divided highway, still in third gear, she asked about the tennis.

"Your father told me you'd just won a big tennis match at Rotherham," she said.

"Roehampton," said Floyd. "Yes, I did."

"He sounded very pleased about it."

"Did he?"

"But then he said you'd decided to take a bit of a break from tennis. He said you'd gotten overtired and needed a rest."

"I'm not taking a break," said Floyd. "I've given up tennis. I'm not going to play anymore."

"Goodness . . ." Granny Plum gave him a sideways glance as she spoke. "Have you told him?"

"Yes," said Floyd. "Several times."

"Did he mind?"

"Yes, he did. Quite a lot."

"Well, I'm not surprised," said Granny Plum. "He's always taken your tennis very seriously." She said this as if it was something that Floyd himself might not have noticed. "But then of course he takes everything seriously. He was like that as a boy. Always very ambitious." She gave a sigh. "I don't know where he got it from. Certainly not from me. I've never taken anything that seriously.

Except possibly food. I take food quite seriously . . . Which reminds me, I thought I'd do a pizza tonight. Do you still eat garlic bread?"

Arriving at Bude, and at the little town house that looked out over the Bude Canal, Floyd's grandmother gave him a plate of freshly baked scones and clotted cream and jam—to welcome him to the West Country, she said—then suggested he take a walk down to the beach while she cooked supper.

The beach was less than two minutes away, and it was a familiar route. Floyd's parents had brought him down here several times in the past, though they normally stayed at the Falcon Hotel when they did, because the hotel had a tennis court, so Floyd could keep up with his training.

He walked along the road, crossed the canal over the lock gates, and then went down the steps onto the sand. The beach was beginning to clear now as families drifted back to their hotels and guesthouses for a bath and an evening meal. The tide was out, and Floyd walked past the lifeboat station and across the sand until he reached some rocks where he sat down and stared out to sea.

He had been there only a few minutes when he realized that, sitting only a few feet away, was Mike. It was a surprise but, curiously, a rather pleasant one, and Floyd found himself smiling at the sight. There was a trace of a smile on Mike's face as well, as he turned to Floyd and gestured briefly out to sea in a movement that plainly said, *Isn't this fantastic!*

Floyd agreed that it was, and the two of them sat there in companionable silence for a while, gazing out at the few remaining children running in and out of the water, at a group of surfers determinedly trying to stand up on waves that were not much more than ripples, and at the gulls screaming overhead.

And at some point as they sat there—Floyd could never quite remember when exactly it happened—he found something inside him had changed. It was, he later told Dr. Pinner, as if he had been carrying a very heavy weight on his back, carrying it for so long that he had ceased to be aware that it even existed, but now, sitting on the rock looking out at the sea, he felt it slide from his shoulders and quietly vanish. Its disappearance left him with a giddy, almost light-headed sense of freedom.

He drew in a long deep breath of sea air and, beside him, Mike finally spoke.

"Thalatta! Thalatta!" he murmured softly, and Floyd was about to ask what that meant when his friend disappeared.

The pattern of Floyd's days that summer was soon set. He would get up at about seven, an hour later than he would have at home, and sit in the kitchen while Granny Plum cooked him breakfast. After that he would help her with some of the household chores. His grandmother had a long list of things that could only be done by someone younger, taller, and stronger than herself, so Floyd would climb a ladder to clear the gutters, carry things up into the attic for storage, dig out a tree stump in the garden . . . but whatever the task, at some point in the middle or late morning, his grandmother would tell him that was enough, remind him he was supposed to be on vacation, and tell him to go off and enjoy himself.

So Floyd would head down to the beach, and from there he would start walking—either north in the direction of Hartland Quay, or south toward Boscastle—and depending on the tide he would either take the path along the cliffs or follow the line of the shore across the sand and the rocks.

When he got hungry, he would stop and eat the sandwiches and drink the bottle of juice that Granny Plum had put in his backpack, and then later he would start walking home again. By the time he got back, he would find his grandmother preparing a supper even larger than his breakfast, and the rest of the evening would be spent in front of the television. Granny Plum was a big fan of the soaps and would keep up a running commentary on the characters while Floyd dozed, or watched with her, or read a book.

• • •

Mike appeared on several occasions during these walks. The first time was when Floyd was making his way along the coastal path near Widemouth. He came over the brow of the hill and there was Mike, a few paces in front of him, his coat blown backward by the breeze, one hand stuffed in the pocket of his jeans and the other pointing out to sea.

Following the line of his finger, Floyd looked down and saw a group of dolphins, no more than a hundred yards from the shoreline, leaping in and out of the water as they moved across the bay.

"They're not dolphins," said Mike.

"No?" Floyd had taken a pair of binoculars from his bag. "So what are they?"

"Page one hundred seventy-three," said Mike with a smile, and again Floyd was about to ask what that meant, when he found that Mike had gone.

That evening, he told his grandmother about seeing the dolphins that weren't dolphins.

"How do you know they weren't?" she asked.

"I don't really," said Floyd, "but there was someone else on the cliff, and he seemed very certain. I might try the library tomorrow and look them up."

Granny Plum said nothing, but burrowed briefly in the bookcase to her right before producing a volume that she passed across. "It'll probably be in there somewhere," she said.

The book was *A Field Guide to the British Shoreline*, and Floyd was about to look in the index to see if it had anything on dolphins when a thought popped into his head and he turned, instead, to page one hundred seventy-three.

There, sure enough, was a short chapter on the distinguishing features of sea mammals that could be seen from the shores of coastal Britain.

"Porpoises," said Floyd. "The things I saw were porpoises."

"Were they, dear?" said his grandmother. "That's nice."

Floyd flipped through some of the other pages in the book. "Could I borrow this?" he asked.

"It's yours," said his grandmother. "Your grandfather gave it to you when you were five. You used to spend hours looking at the pictures."

• • •

The *Field Guide* accompanied Floyd on all his walks after that. From it, he learned the names of some of the varieties of bivalve that were glued in the millions to the rocks. He learned about the different types of seaweed, so that he could tell the difference between thongweed and dabberlocks, and he took to carrying a trowel as well as the *Field Guide* so that he could dig in the sand for beach worms and amphipods. As the weeks passed, he spent less of his time walking and more of it crouched over a rock pool, or studying the debris of marine life that had been washed up along the shoreline.

When Mike appeared, it was usually to point out something that Floyd might otherwise have missed. It was Mike, for instance, who pointed out the impressively toothsome jaws of an anglerfish lying bleached among the debris left by the tide. And it was Mike who, on the beach at Holacombe, pointed out a turtle, a genuine sea turtle, walking casually across the sand down to the sea before swimming away.

And it was Mike, of course, who led to his meeting with Charity.

It was late afternoon, almost three weeks after his vacation had started, and Floyd was walking back to Bude from Morwenstow when he saw Mike just ahead of him, kneeling on the sand, peering into a rock pool. Floyd came over to join him and found his friend staring at a fish floating on the surface of the water.

It was dead, washed there by the tide, but Floyd was puzzled as to what it was. His *Field Guide* had given him a good working knowledge of most of the things to be found on the shoreline, but it did not cover fish, like this one, that presumably came from deeper waters.

"So what is it?" he asked the figure beside him, but the voice that answered was not Mike's.

"No idea," it said.

The person kneeling on the sand beside him, Floyd realized, was not Mike, but a girl. She had short dark hair, a quizzical look on her face, a small yellow bikini, and she was looking intently at the fish.

"I'll ask Dad," she said. "He'll know."

Standing up, the girl turned and called to a man crouched over a different pool a dozen yards away. "Dad? Look at this!"

The man came over, glanced briefly at Floyd, then bent down to study the dead fish. "Interesting." He spoke in a soft American accent. "You ever seen one of these before?"

Floyd shook his head. "Never. And it's not in my book."

"I'm not surprised. It's not really a shoreline creature. It's an amberjack. You can tell it's a young one from those wavy lines on its side." The man pointed to a tear in the fish's mouth. "Probably caught by a fisherman earlier today. He threw it back in the sea for some reason, and it got washed here by the tide." He stood up. "My turn to show you something now."

He led the way back to the rock pool he had been studying earlier and pointed. "Any idea what that is?"

His finger indicated a starfish, not much more than a quarter inch across, covered in tiny spots.

Floyd studied it carefully. "It's a cushion star, isn't it?"

"It is." The man nodded approvingly. "Do you know what kind?"

Floyd admitted that he didn't.

"It's *Asterina phylactica*," said the girl. "If it was *Asterina gibbosa* it would be bigger and wouldn't have the little spots." She grinned. "But I only know that because Dad just told me."

The man, Floyd learned, was Dr. Richard Lamont, and he was a marine biologist from Boston in the United States, on vacation with his family. The girl in the yellow bikini was his daughter, and his wife was somewhere farther up the beach, lying on a towel, reading a book. Dr. Lamont seemed to know even more about marine life than the *Field Guide*, and for nearly an hour they sat and talked about some of the things they had found, and some of the things they had hoped to find but hadn't yet. Dr. Lamont was particularly intrigued to hear about the turtle Floyd had seen in the bay near Holacombe and agreed, from his description, that it had indeed probably been a loggerhead.

It was the first time Floyd had spoken to anyone apart from his grandmother since coming to Cornwall, and he enjoyed it. It was interesting to talk to someone who knew so much about marine life, and interesting, too, to be with the girl. Her name was Charity. She was almost exactly the same age as himself and . . . it was a very small bikini.

When Charity's father announced that it was time they were getting back to their hotel, Floyd felt a stab of disappointment, and then was curiously pleased when the girl asked if he would be around the next day.

"We normally come down to the beach after lunch," she said, "and stay for a couple of hours. We might see you again, if you're around then."

And Floyd agreed that they might.

The next day, Floyd did not walk as far as usual. He went north to Steeple Point, but then turned around and was back at the beach at Bude by one o'clock, sitting on the breakwater looking out over the sands at the retreating tide.

The wind had veered around to the north, bringing down a layer of clouds, and the resulting drop in temperature meant there were fewer people on the beach. Those who had braved the chill were mostly wrapped in coats or sweaters, but none of them was Charity and, an hour and a half later, there was still no sign of her.

Floyd had actually decided there was no point waiting any longer and that he might as well go home when he saw Mike standing at the edge of the surf, the waves almost washing over his shoes.

Floyd walked across the sand to join him. He half expected his friend to point out some rare animal or plant, but all Mike said was . . .

"You need to wait."

"For Charity?"

Mike nodded. "And when she gets here, you should tell her about me."

"Oh . . . Are you sure?"

Mike did not answer, but gazed calmly at the horizon.

"It's just I was thinking," said Floyd, "that if I tell her about you, she'll probably think I'm crazy."

"Possibly," Mike agreed. "But you should still tell her."

"All right," said Floyd. "If she ever turns up I will, but I wouldn't mind knowing how long I'll have to wait because . . ."

He was interrupted at that moment by a shout and turned to see Charity running across the sand toward them.

"Sorry I'm late," she said a little breathlessly when she reached him. "We got stuck in Tintagel. Dad was giving a talk and everyone kept asking him questions and . . . anyway, I'm glad you're still here." She smiled, and at that exact moment the clouds parted and the sun came out. "Do you want to go for a walk or something?"

"Great," said Floyd, but looked at Charity's shoes and her dress. Both were rather formal.

"I know," she said. "I need to get changed first. And I need to tell my parents where we're going, and I need to grab some lunch, but I promise I'll be back here in ten minutes. Can you wait that long?"

Floyd agreed that he would wait.

"I thought, if it's not too far, you could show me where you found the turtle," said Charity. "Your friend can come too if he likes."

"My friend?"

"The boy you were talking to just now," said Charity. "Long black coat? Dark, curly hair?"

"You saw him?" Floyd could not hide his surprise.

"He was with you yesterday as well, wasn't he?" said Charity. "But then he went away as I came over." She smiled up at him. "You're not going to run away too, are you? In the next ten minutes?"

"Absolutely not," said Floyd.

• • •

Charity was back, changed and clutching a bag of sandwiches, in slightly less than ten minutes, and Floyd took her to the beach where he had seen the loggerhead turtle.

Although the turtle was not there, they found the marks of its movement in the sand above the high-tide mark, so they sat at the base of the cliffs with the sun in their faces to wait for a while in case it returned.

They sat side by side, Charity leaning her body against Floyd's for shelter from the wind, and they talked. Charity talked about her home in Boston, her school, and her father's work for the university, and Floyd talked about Sheffield and about tennis and, finally, about Mike.

He told Charity how his friend had first appeared, about the match when he had first stepped onto the court, and how Floyd had then discovered that no one else could see him. He told her about the trips to Dr. Pinner, about projection and about what had happened at the championship at Roehampton. It was a long story, and all the time he was telling it, Charity spoke hardly a word. She sat beside him with her chin on her knees and listened.

"So," she said when the story was finally over, "you are, at this moment, the best under-eighteen tennis player in the U.K., right?"

"Right," said Floyd.

"But you're not going to play tennis anymore, because Mike doesn't want to."

"Well . . ."

"Even though he's not a real person."

"No . . . well, he is . . . sort of. But only to me."

"So why could I see him?"

"I don't know."

"He's not here now, is he?" Charity looked hopefully around the beach.

"No," said Floyd, "not at the moment."

"That's a pity." Charity sighed.

"Is it?"

"Oh, yes." Charity was looking out to sea. "I quite fancied him, you know."

• • •

On the way back to Bude, Charity said her parents had suggested she invite Floyd to join them for dinner that night at the hotel.

"Only if you're not busy or anything," she added.

"I'm not busy exactly," said Floyd. "But my grandmother will have cooked a meal and I . . . could we do it tomorrow?"

"I'm going home tomorrow," said Charity. "We're flying back to Boston."

Floyd absorbed this information, and also absorbed the fact that somehow he and Charity were now holding hands as they walked.

"I'm sure Gran won't mind," he said. "I'll just go home and tell her."

Floyd's grandmother did not mind at all, though she did insist on walking with Floyd to the Falcon Hotel that evening and being introduced to Charity and her parents. Charity's mother invited her to join them for dinner as well, but Granny Plum declined. There was a particularly exciting story line on *Eastenders* that week, she said, and she needed to get back.

At dinner, there was a certain amount of talk about tennis but much more about fish. Floyd talked about his tanks of tropical fish at home, and Charity's parents talked about how they had studied many of the same fish in their natural habitats on the reefs of the Caribbean or around the atolls of the South Pacific. Charity's mother, it turned out, was a marine photographer whose specialty was larger sea mammals. At the time, she was working on pictures for a book about beaked whales, and both she and her husband had an endless supply of stories of strange discoveries, near disasters, and weird accidents.

After dinner, Charity said she wanted to take one last walk along the beach, and Floyd offered to go with her. The tide was in and they walked in bare feet through the surf in the moonlit warmth of the night and Floyd realized that he was happy. Happy in a way that he had not been since the whole business with Mike had started, and as he held Charity in his arms, the impossible happened.

For a good half hour, he didn't think about tennis or invisible friends at all.

Three days later, Floyd went home.

His grandmother drove him to the train at Exeter, and there were tears in her eyes as she hugged him good-bye, told him for the umpteenth time how wonderful it had been to have him to stay, and made him promise to come back as soon as he could.

Coming home was not quite as difficult as Floyd had feared. His parents asked at supper that night if he had changed his mind about playing tennis but did not seem particularly surprised when Floyd said that he hadn't.

"Well, you know what we think," his father had said. "But it's your decision and we won't try and make you change it. If you *do* decide differently, though, anytime in the next year or so, it's not too late. Not by a long way."

His parents kept their promise and the subject of tennis was not mentioned again, which was a relief, but it still was not easy. It felt very strange to be at home but never going out to the court in the backyard, never going off to training sessions before and after school, never spending long hours practicing volleys and serves and backhands, never even picking up a racket.

It was not just strange at home either. Schoolwork had never held much importance in Floyd's life—good grades are not needed to become a tennis champion—and the whole business of reading, studying, and writing essays was not something to which he had given any particular attention. Now, however, it was necessary that he did.

Charity was the one who had persuaded him that it *was* necessary. She had suggested that it might be kind of fun if they went to college together and, in some of the emails she sent him on an almost daily basis from America, would remind him that this would only be possible if he passed his exams.

So he began to take schoolwork seriously. There were still nine months to go before he took his exams, and he asked his teachers what he needed to do to catch up, worked out a timetable, and . . . got on with it. It wasn't, he discovered, all that different from preparing for a tennis competition. In fact, compared with getting up at six and practicing backhands for two hours, schoolwork was a lot less demanding.

In her messages, Charity asked occasionally about Mike, wanting to know if he had reappeared at all, but the answer was always the same. There had been no sign of him since the day on the beach when he had told Floyd to wait, and as the months passed, Floyd began to think that perhaps this time his friend had disappeared for good.

• • •

Then one evening in early December, when Floyd was coming out of the main library in Sheffield—his English teacher had told him he should try to read at least one novel a week—he saw Mike standing on the sidewalk on the opposite side of the road.

Mike gave a little nod of greeting and, gesturing for Floyd to follow, set off briskly down the street. Floyd had to wait for a gap in the traffic before running across to join him, and by that time Mike was fifty yards farther ahead. Floyd followed him as he turned left, then right, then left again, always staying about the same distance ahead, and they had been traveling like this for a good ten minutes when Mike stopped. He looked back to check that Floyd was watching, before entering one of the buildings. Floyd hurried up to the spot and found himself in front of a doorway with a sign above it that said:

NEWLY OPENED! WATERWORLD!
THE PERFECT FAMILY OUTING! Admission £3.50.

When Floyd stepped inside, there was no sign of Mike, only a bored-looking girl in the booth waiting for him to pay his money. Floyd gave her three pounds fifty, took the ticket, walked in and found himself in a corridor with glass tanks running from floor to ceiling on either side of him. The tanks were lit from inside, and the fish they contained were interesting variants of the ones he had at home. Floyd, however, ignored them and pressed on, looking for Mike. He walked to the end of the corridor, which led to another corridor containing more tanks, and then into another and . . . halted. Ahead of him, a man on a stepladder was lowering a plastic bag containing several fish into the top of one of the tanks.

"No! Stop!" Floyd found himself calling out without thinking. "You can't put those in there!"

The man ignored him.

Floyd stepped closer. "Honestly . . . If you put them in there, you'll kill them."

The man looked at him. "They're fish," he said. "They're not going to drown."

"I know," said Floyd, "but those are saltwater fish. And judging by the species you've already got in there, that is a tank of freshwater."

Slowly, the man pulled the bag out of the water and thought for a moment. "Chief!" he called, and he stood there, looking at Floyd and waiting.

An elderly man in an old-fashioned suit and with an old-fashioned drooping mustache appeared. He gazed quizzically up at the man with the fish, who pointed to Floyd.

"He says if I put these fish in the tank, it'll kill them."

"They're green puffers," said Floyd. "They live in brackish water. If you put them in freshwater, they'll die."

The Chief did not answer immediately. Instead he reached into a pocket of his jacket and took out a well-thumbed copy of *The Handbook of Tropical Fish*. He turned the pages slowly, found the place he wanted, and passed the book to Floyd. A finger pointed carefully to one of the pictures.

"That's a Congo puffer," said Floyd. "The ones in that bag are green puffers." He flicked quickly to the back of the book, turned the pages, and passed it back to the Chief. "See? They're both spotted, and they look very similar, but one lives in freshwater, one in salt. Those are green puffers and they need to be in salt water."

The Chief carefully studied both pictures in his book,

and then the fish in the bag. Finally, he turned to the man on the ladder.

"Put them in tank number four," he said, then looked thoughtfully at Floyd. "You got a minute?"

"What for?"

"Like to show you something."

Without waiting for a reply, he turned and led the way down the hall between the tanks. Floyd followed him as he turned right and then left before stopping in front of a large tank containing three or four dead cherubfish bobbing gently on the surface in the bubbles from the oxygenator.

"Lost twelve fish in this tank in two days," said the Chief. "Just . . . died. Any idea why?"

Floyd peered closely at the tank. "You've got aiptasia."

"Got what?"

"Aiptasia," repeated Floyd. "Those anemones on the bottom. They've got a poisonous sting. There's various ways to get rid of them, but the safest thing is to throw everything out, sterilize the tank, and start again."

The Chief pulled thoughtfully at his mustache and stared at the dead cherubfish for several seconds before turning back to Floyd.

"You want a job?" he asked.

It was seeing Mike again that made Floyd decide it was time to contact Dr. Pinner. He was not worried exactly—the appearance of his invisible friend no longer bothered him in the way that it had six months before—but he did want to know *why* Mike had come back, and Dr. Pinner was the only person Floyd could think of who might have the answer.

When he got home, he dug out the letter the psychologist had written at the start of the summer, found the email address he had given, and tapped out a brief message on his laptop. He didn't go into detail, simply saying that Mike had reappeared that day outside the library, and that he would like to talk about it if that was possible. He was not at all sure that the psychologist would remember his promise or that he would still be willing to reply, but in fact it was barely half an hour later that his father pushed open the door to his room.

"Dr. Pinner just called," he said. "He says you've seen Mike again."

"Yes," said Floyd. "I was going to tell you at supper."

"So what happened?"

"Nothing really." Floyd shrugged. "After school I went to the library, and when I came out Mike was standing on the other side of the road."

"What did he want?"

"He didn't say." Floyd gave what he hoped was a reassuring smile. "It's all right. He wasn't trying to persuade me to murder anyone. But I thought it might be good to talk to Dr. Pinner. If that's all right?"

His father nodded, but with no real enthusiasm. "He says he'll be at the Sheridan Hotel tomorrow at four o'clock."

"Really?"

"I asked him how much it would cost, but he said he wasn't coming as a therapist. Just as a friend."

"Oh."

"But I told him if you ever felt you had to go back to him, you know, for more of those sessions and things, we could . . . we could probably pay for them."

"Right," said Floyd. "Thank you."

There was a long silence while his father stood in the doorway, staring down at the carpet.

"I don't know why," he said, before turning to leave, "but everything was a lot easier when you were ten."

• • •

The Sheridan Hotel was only a short walk from school, and Floyd found Dr. Pinner waiting in the hotel lounge with a pot of tea and a plate of cake already on the table in front of him.

"So," he said cheerfully as they settled into their chairs, "Mike came back?"

"He's come back a few times, actually," said Floyd. "I saw him while I was on vacation in the summer, as well."

"Oh, yes?" said the psychologist. "I would very much like to hear about that."

For the next forty minutes, he listened closely while Floyd described what had happened when Mike had appeared outside the library the day before, and then went through each of the times he had appeared in Cornwall, and finally—because it was a part of the story the psychologist had not heard before—about Mike's appearance in the locker rooms at Roehampton before the match against Barrington Gates. It was the first time Floyd had shared these details with anyone apart from Charity, and describing it all was a sharp reminder of how odd the whole story was.

Dr. Pinner, however, did not seem to be bothered by any oddness. All he said, and he used the phrase a good many times, was how interesting it all was.

"*Very* interesting," he repeated, when Floyd had finished. "It is a remarkable story."

"So do you think I should be worried?" asked Floyd.

"Worried?" Dr. Pinner looked at him over the top of his teacup. "Why? You're not worried, are you?"

"Not exactly," said Floyd. "But I am . . . puzzled. About what Mike wants. And why I'm still seeing him."

Dr. Pinner gave a little shrug. "I should imagine that there are still things he wants to tell you."

"Like what?"

Dr. Pinner made a gesture with his hands. "I'm sure he'll make that clear. In time."

Floyd considered this.

"You still think Mike is a part of me?"

"Oh, yes," said Dr. Pinner, and then added, "though I'm beginning to wonder if it might not be more accurate to say that *you* are a part of *him*."

"Seriously?"

"Doesn't it seem that way to you?" The psychologist helped himself to another slice of cake. "I mean, he's the one who seems to *know* things, isn't he? He's the one who's telling you what to look out for, where to go, what to do . . ."

"I suppose." Floyd frowned. "But *how* does he know those things? I mean, how did he know the difference between a porpoise and a dolphin? Or that I should look on page one hundred seventy-three of a book I haven't opened since I was five? And how come Charity could see him? Because she did. She described him perfectly."

"I know!" Dr. Pinner was nodding sympathetically. "And how can he speak Greek and quote Xenophon? It is all most mysterious!"

Floyd's frown deepened. "He speaks Greek? When did he do that?"

"*Thalatta* is the Greek word for the sea," said Dr. Pinner. "And '*Thalatta! Thalatta!*' is a famous quotation from Xenophon."

"Who's Xenophon?" asked Floyd.

"He was a soldier," Dr. Pinner explained. "One of the leaders of a Greek army that invaded Persia in about 400 B.C. They got cut off and Xenophon found himself leading these thousands of men through deserts and mountains with no idea where they were going. They were completely lost, until one day they got to the sea . . . and Xenophon triumphantly shouted, '*Thalatta! Thalatta!*' because that's when he knew they'd be all right."

"Did he? Why?"

"Because once they'd found the sea, all they had to do to get back to Greece was follow the line of the coast. There were still plenty of battles and fighting and hard journeys ahead of them, of course, but the point was they weren't lost anymore. Finding the sea meant Xenophon knew that the army would get home."

There was a long moment of silence while Floyd thought about this.

"Can I ask," said Dr. Pinner, "if you took the job? At Waterworld?"

"I said I'd think about it," said Floyd. "I'm not sure it's a good idea, though. I've got a lot of work to catch up on at school and . . ."

Dr. Pinner did not let him finish the sentence. He reached across the table and put a hand on Floyd's arm to emphasize his next words.

"Take the job," he said. "Trust me on this one, Floyd. Take the job."

If, as Dr. Pinner believed, Mike's words on the shore at Bude had somehow meant to imply that Floyd had reached a place from which, like Xenophon, he could safely navigate his way home, that was certainly not how it felt. Not to Floyd anyway. It was more than two years before he saw Mike again, and they were years when, far from being triumphantly sure of the direction he needed to go, Floyd felt increasingly uncertain and . . . lost.

He felt lost at home, watching his parents' sadness as they slowly came to accept that their son had meant it when he said that he never wanted to play tennis again. Floyd's father kept his word, and neither he nor his mother ever attempted to persuade him to change his mind, but their unspoken disappointment was not easily hidden or ignored. The pain of that decision was something they all still felt on an almost daily basis.

He felt lost, too, at school, or at least that he was somehow still not in the right place. He achieved respectable grades that were more than enough to get him on the college track, but schoolwork was never something Floyd found very satisfying. Sitting at a desk, studying, was not how he wanted to spend his life, any more than he wanted to spend it on a tennis court, and sometime during the school year he decided that he would not be applying to college. The thought of another four years spent reading books and writing essays was more than he could face.

The main appeal of going to college of course had been the idea of going there with Charity, but that relationship had somehow gotten lost as well. He and Charity had hoped to meet up in the summer after Floyd had taken his exams, but it hadn't happened. Charity's planned trip to the U.K. with her mother had fallen through at the last minute, when Mrs. Lamont was hospitalized with an infection she caught while photographing a whale carcass. Charity suggested that Floyd come to America instead, and he was all set to do so until he discovered that his passport had expired and there was no time to get a new one.

Instead, he stayed in Sheffield that summer and fell into a relationship with a girl called Sandra Drickett—someone he knew from the Sandown tennis club. He mentioned Sandra to Charity in one of his emails and, soon after that, the messages to and from America began to taper off. From writing almost every day, they switched to emails once a week, then once a month. The relationship with Sandra didn't last very long but, by the time it was over, Charity was mailing that she had started going out with a basketball player from her physics class, and after that the messaging became even less regular and there was no more talk of a visit to the U.K.

The one part of his life where Floyd did not feel lost, where in fact he felt completely at home, was at Waterworld. He had, on Dr. Pinner's advice, taken the job that the Chief had offered him and, from a few hours a week at the start, the work grew into something that came to absorb almost all of his free time. It was, despite the minimal pay, without doubt the most satisfying part of Floyd's life.

The pay was minimal because Waterworld did not make a profit. The Chief's real income came from various businesses he owned around Sheffield—Floyd never knew what they were—and he had set up Waterworld to indulge an enthusiasm rather than with any expectation of making money. The cost of heating and lighting the tanks, combined with the cost of buying the fish and feeding them, always meant that Waterworld ran at a loss.

Almost the only thing Floyd knew about the Chief, apart from the fact that he came originally from somewhere in West Pakistan, was that he had a passionate interest in anything that lived in the water. The fact that Floyd shared the same enthusiasm meant that, from the start, he was treated more as a partner than an employee. Most days, as Floyd busied himself cleaning tanks or checking oxygen levels, the stooping figure of the Chief would appear at some point, wanting to show him something in a catalog or discuss a possible purchase or talk about what combination of fish in which tank would make the most effective display. Fish and the aquarium were the Chief's great obsession and, in the two and a half years that Floyd worked for him, he could only remember one occasion when the two of them talked about anything else.

It was a Saturday, in the Easter break before his exams, when the Chief appeared at Floyd's shoulder, asking if he had a moment, before leading the way up to his tiny office on the second floor.

"Wanted to show you that," he said, pointing to a ledger lying open on the desk.

The ledger, carefully filled in by hand, contained the details of the income and expenditure involved in running Waterworld for the last month, and Floyd was surprised to see that the business had, for the first time, made a small profit.

"Wow," he said. "Nearly three pounds. What are we going to spend it on?"

"Might not be a lot," the Chief agreed, "but . . . still good. And mostly thanks to you. Stuff you do with the kids."

It had been Floyd's idea, some months before, to offer "tours" of the attractions in Waterworld. He had worked out a half-hour talk that showed visitors things like an electric eel stunning its prey before eating it, and demonstrating the power in the suckers of an octopus by allowing the arms to close on his fist, before peeling them off. The tour had been particularly popular with children, and recently some teachers had been bringing in classes from the local schools.

"What you going to do, Floyd?" The Chief was sitting at his desk, looking thoughtfully up at him as he spoke. "When you leave school?"

The question took Floyd by surprise. Not because he hadn't thought about it, but because it was not something he had ever expected the Chief to ask.

"I don't know," he said. "I've been wondering about it myself recently, but . . . I don't know."

The Chief nodded, as if this was no more than he had expected.

"Could continue working here," he said. "Glad to have you. You know that. But . . . not what you really want, is it?"

The possibility of working permanently at Waterworld was something that had crossed Floyd's mind, but the Chief was right. It was *not* what he really wanted, even if the pay had been raised to something more than minimal. He enjoyed the work, and he appreciated the way it had meant he was not entirely dependent on his parents, but the thought of spending the rest of his life indoors, even surrounded by tanks of fish, was almost as alarming as having to spend his life on a tennis court.

"No, it's not," he said. "I mean, I love working here, Chief, but, no . . . it's not what I want to do forever."

The chief nodded thoughtfully.

"So what is it?" he asked. "That you *really* want to do?"

"Well, that's the problem," said Floyd. "I don't know that either."

"Should think about it." The Chief waved an admonishing finger. "Good thing to know. What you really want."

And Floyd could only agree that knowing what he really wanted to do in life would be a very good thing indeed.

• • •

"The trouble is," he told Dr. Pinner three days later as they sat having tea and cake in the Sheridan Hotel, "I have no idea. I don't even know what *sort* of job I'd like, let alone whether I'd be able to get it even if I did."

He and the psychologist were sitting at their usual table at the hotel. They had taken to meeting there every month or so, originally to talk about Mike and to hear if he had appeared again for any reason, but these days mostly to talk about life and what Floyd was doing. He found the meetings oddly comforting, chiefly because he was able to talk to Dr. Pinner about the things that bothered him in a way that he could not talk to anyone else. Least of all his parents.

"I don't think you need to worry about all that at the moment," said Dr. Pinner. "You concentrate on your exams. That's all you have to think about for now."

"But I *do* worry," said Floyd. His exams were in a little over three weeks and he worried a lot, not so much about the tests as about what would follow.

"I'm not going to college, so in a couple of months I'm going to have to get a job of some sort and I don't even know where to start looking. I can stay at Waterworld for a bit, but the Chief's right. It's not what I really want to do. And what sort of an idiot am I if I've given up tennis, which could at least have made me a lot of money even though I didn't want to do it, so I could take a job doing something I still don't want to do but earns me hardly anything at all?"

"Most people your age don't know what they want to do," said Dr. Pinner. "It's all right. When the time comes, something will turn up."

"Why? Why should you think that 'something will turn up'?"

"Because in my experience it always does," said Dr. Pinner. "And you have less to worry about than most of us, don't you? Because you have Mike."

"But I don't!" Floyd protested. "Mike's been no help at all! I haven't seen him for over two years!"

"Not seeing him is a good sign, isn't it?" argued Dr. Pinner. "I mean, if you were off track in any way, or not doing something you should be doing, I suspect he'd let you know about it in very short order."

"Why? Why do you think that?"

"Because it seems to be what he does." Dr. Pinner poured himself some more tea. "Honestly, as far as I can see, you really don't need to worry!"

• • •

Dr. Pinner might think there was no cause to worry and that, when it came down to it, Mike would ensure that Floyd was somehow nudged onto the right path, but Floyd himself was not convinced. More than two years had passed without any sign of his "friend," and he privately doubted that he would ever see him again.

But it turned out Dr. Pinner was right. Mike did come back and give another nudge, though not in quite the manner or in the direction that either Floyd or the psychologist had expected.

The day after he finished his last exam, Floyd got an email from Charity. It was the first message he had had from her in several weeks, and it said that she and her father would be stopping over in London for a couple of days in the second week of July, on their way to a marine ecology conference in Venice, and she wondered if he might be free to meet up.

The day she suggested, a Tuesday, was coincidentally the day Floyd's parents were driving down to London to watch the quarterfinals of the women's tennis at Wimbledon. Mr. and Mrs. Beresford did not normally go to Wimbledon these days, but that year they had been given tickets by a couple from the Sandown tennis club.

Unexpectedly unable to travel themselves, and with a ten-year-old daughter, Sissie, who had been looking forward to the trip since before Christmas, they had asked the Beresfords to take her instead. Floyd traveled down to London with them in the car.

The two weeks of Wimbledon were a tricky time in the Beresford household. When he was younger, Floyd's parents would have bought tickets themselves for at least one of the days, and the family would have watched as many of the other matches as possible on television. Now, when the television was on, Floyd did his best to keep out of the way. There was, inevitably, a certain tension in the air.

The tension was particularly high this year because Barrington Gates had just hit the big time. He had done unexpectedly well in several international tournaments and was now the U.K.'s number one seed and officially the Great British Hope. All through the first week of Wimbledon, his face was to be seen on the covers of a score of magazines, and there were pieces written about him on an almost daily basis in the papers. Any time his name was mentioned on the news there was a sort of heavy silence in the Beresford house, and although nobody said anything Floyd knew what his parents were thinking.

Barrington Gates is number one now . . . and you were so much better than him . . . It should be you out there . . .

• • •

His parents dropped Floyd off at the train station at Wimbledon and, while they made their way to the place they had booked in one of the parking lots, he caught a train into central London.

He walked the last part of his journey to the hotel in Russell Square where Charity and her father were staying, and was slightly taken aback by the elegant figure who came forward to greet him in the hotel lobby, looking alarmingly grown-up and self-possessed.

"Dad's still on the phone upstairs," said Charity. "But he said to go in and get started. He'll be down as soon as he can."

She led the way into the dining room, where the waiter showed them to a table by the window. They sat opposite each other, and Floyd asked politely if she was looking forward to the conference in Venice.

"Well, I'm looking forward to Venice," said Charity, "but I'm not going to the actual conference. I'm just here to make sure Dad shows up at the right place and in a clean shirt. How did your exams go?"

Floyd told her about his exams and then asked about Charity's plans for college, and they were still at the stage of making polite conversation when Dr. Lamont appeared. His hair was a little grayer than Floyd remembered, but he shook hands briskly before turning to Charity.

"Have you told him yet?"

"No," said Charity. "Not yet."

"Told me what?"

"Dad wants to offer you a job." Charity was carefully studying the menu.

"It's not exactly a job," her father explained. "I'm doing a project in the Gulf of Mexico for three months next year, looking at the causes of hypoxia. You know anything about that?"

"The fall in oxygen levels that kills fish?" said Floyd.

"That's right." Dr. Lamont nodded. "We'll be working from a research vessel that the university charters, trying to find which factors cause the most damage."

Floyd looked across at Charity. "Are you going?"

"Charity will be at college by then," said Dr. Lamont. "She starts at Cornell in the fall. But she tells me you're taking a gap year, is that right?"

That was, Floyd admitted, one way of putting it.

"So . . ." Dr. Lamont paused to ask a waiter to bring him a beer. "You need to understand it won't be a vacation. It's not a large ship. We have room for six scientists, and the others will all be graduates or PhD students. I'm inviting you because sometimes it's useful to have a gofer helping out with the chores—cleaning, looking after the equipment, fetching and carrying... That's what the job would be. Along with doing whatever anyone tells you to do."

"Right..."

"Are you qualified as a scuba diver?"

"No," said Floyd.

"Well, you'd need to get your Open Water Diver certificate. You wouldn't be much use to us unless you could dive, and we couldn't let you dive without it. And obviously you'll have to sort out a visa. You'd need to get to that pretty soon. It can take a bit longer these days."

"Yes..."

"We give you a bunk and as much food as you can eat, but no money. There isn't the budget to pay you. Might be a few dollars in your pocket at the end, but don't count on it." He paused. "So... are you interested?"

Floyd wasn't sure he *was* interested in being a gofer. The idea of being on a boat in the Gulf of Mexico sounded like it might be fun, but temporary work like this was not going to solve the problem of what he was going to do for the rest of his life. He wondered why Dr. Lamont had thought he *would* be interested, and was about to say that it was very kind but no thanks when he glanced across at Charity.

She was staring through the window at the street outside as if she had no particular interest in Floyd's reply to her father's offer, but he suddenly knew that the only reason Dr. Lamont was offering him the job was that Charity had asked him to. She was the one who had persuaded her father to make the offer and, however much she tried not to show it, she very much wanted Floyd to take it. How he knew this and why Charity had done it, he had no idea, but the realization was enough to make him decide not to turn down the offer straight off.

"Thank you," he said. "Would you mind if I took a bit of time to think it over? I probably ought to talk to my parents about it, as well."

"Of course." Dr. Lamont took a piece of paper from his jacket. "These are the dates. If you do decide to come, I'll need to know by the start of September and you'll need to be in Boston by January fourth. The project finishes April second, and after that you can either fly straight back to the U.K. or you could spend a few days with us. Take a vacation."

"I'd be home then." Charity was looking at him now and the smile was back. "Easter vacation. I could show you around Boston."

"Oh," said Floyd. "That'd be good."

Dr. Lamont had to leave halfway through lunch—he was giving a lecture on algal toxins at University College—but he told Floyd and Charity to stay as long as they liked and to order whatever they wanted, and then left.

The two of them sat and talked for nearly three hours. They talked about Bude, about going and not going to college, about Sandra Drickett and Charity's basketball-playing boyfriend, and, somewhere along the line, Charity stopped being alarmingly confident and sophisticated, and became instead the girl who had walked beside him along a beach in Cornwall.

When it was time to leave—Floyd had arranged with his parents to be back at Wimbledon by five—the last thing Charity said was that she hoped he would seriously consider taking the job with her father in January.

And Floyd promised that he would.

It was while waiting at the entrance to the Wimbledon
parking lot, where he had arranged to meet his parents,
that Floyd saw Mike.

He was standing on the opposite sidewalk, still wear-
ing his long black coat despite the warmth of the day and
staring thoughtfully up the road. Floyd smiled at the
sight, and he was about to cross over to join him when
Mike held up a hand, clearly indicating that he should
stay where he was. He was still looking up the road as he
did so, as if waiting for someone to appear, and Floyd
looked up the road as well but saw only the usual stream
of traffic.

The two of them waited like that for almost a minute, and Floyd was just thinking he would cross the road anyway when two things happened. One was that Mike vanished as suddenly and completely as he had appeared, and the other was that he heard a voice calling his name.

"Floyd? Floyd, is that you?"

He found himself looking down at a car that had pulled up in front of him. It was a BMW convertible with cream leather seats, driven by a girl with long blonde hair and an extremely short skirt. The speaker, however, was the young man in the passenger seat.

"It *is* you, isn't it?" The man, dressed in a pair of designer jeans and an immaculately ironed shirt, stepped out of the car. "I knew it. You haven't changed a bit!" Smiling broadly, he took off his dark glasses and Floyd finally recognized who it was.

It was Barrington. Barrington Gates.

"How are you? What are you doing here?" Barrington's smile was getting broader by the second. "Have you got time for a drink?"

"Not really. I'm meeting my parents," said Floyd.

"They're watching a game?"

Floyd nodded. "The Alice Webber match."

"That's only just started." Barrington looked at his watch. "They got held up by rain. You've got half an hour even if she gets whitewashed. Come on! You and me have a lot to talk about!"

"Honey?" The girl in the car sounded rather bored. "You're going to be late for practice."

"Who cares about that?" Barrington turned to face her. "This is Floyd! Floyd Beresford!"

The girl looked up. "The guy from Roehampton?"

Barrington nodded.

"Hey!" The girl's skirt rose even higher up her thighs as she leaned across to hold out a hand. "I've heard about you."

"Come on . . ." Barrington put an arm on Floyd's shoulder. "One drink . . ."

"I'm not sure, I . . ."

"There's no point arguing!" The girl in the car was looking up at Floyd with a dazzling smile. "He's not going to let you go now he's found you. But try not to keep him too long! He really does need to practice." She looked at Barrington. "See you on the courts in half an hour!"

As the car moved forward into the parking lot, Floyd found himself led across the road toward the Members' Entrance to the Wimbledon grounds, with Barrington asking how he was, how his parents were, and what on earth he was doing these days. There was a slight delay when Barrington had to stop and sign his autograph for a group of schoolgirls, and another while he had a word with the security man before Floyd was allowed in, but then he was being led down a long corridor lined with photographs of past Wimbledon winners and up some stairs into a comfortable lounge area with tables and a bar.

"You're working in an aquarium?" Barrington led the way to a table in the corner. "Really?"

"Really," said Floyd.

"I suppose I shouldn't be surprised." Barrington looked at him. "You always did have a thing about fish, didn't you? There was a story that your parents bought you one every time you won a match. Was that true?"

Floyd admitted that it was, though he was surprised that Barrington knew about it.

"Oh, there were a lot of stories floating around about you," said Barrington. "About what you liked and what you didn't. Everyone wanted to know!"

"Did they?"

"Of course!" Barrington smiled. "You were the one we were all worried about, weren't you? We were always swapping stories about you. That's why I was trying to psych you out in the locker room that day." His smile widened. "That didn't work out too well for me, did it!"

He paused to ask a waiter to bring over a large bottle of Perrier and two glasses.

"Look, I have to ask . . . What happened? I mean, you were so *good*, and then . . . How could you give it all up to . . . to work in an aquarium?"

Floyd was confused. This was not the Barrington he remembered. This was not the sneering youth who had made him so angry in the locker room almost three years before. There was no arrogance, no trace of condescension, just an apparently genuine curiosity.

"There was a rumor"—Barrington was still talking—"after you disappeared off the circuit, that you'd had a row with your dad. And another story that you'd had a breakdown because he'd pushed you too hard. But nobody really knew. And your dad never said anything."

"It wasn't anything to do with my father," said Floyd. "I . . . I just didn't want to play tennis anymore."

Barrington frowned. "Even after that last match?"

"I'd decided to stop before then," said Floyd. "I only finished the tournament because my parents wanted me to."

"I see . . ." Barrington leaned back in his chair. "Well . . . no, actually, I don't see at all, but . . . You know they still talk about that match? When I go down to Roehampton— to give a talk to kids or something—even now, I can guarantee that someone will come up to me and say, 'You know that guy who beat you in the Under-18s? What happened to him? He could have been *really* good!'"

"I'm sorry . . . ," said Floyd.

"Nothing to be sorry about. It was the best thing that ever happened to me."

"Was it?" Floyd was puzzled.

"That match . . ." Barrington stopped for a moment to choose his words carefully before continuing. "Up to then, tennis was just, you know, something I seemed to be able to do and that got me in with girls . . . but playing you that day made me realize I hadn't even started. You were just . . . it was like *all* of you was out there. Every single drop of you was out on that court and utterly determined to win. And I realized I'd never concentrated that way on anything. And I knew that if I wanted to win—and that was the game that made me realize how *much* I wanted to win—I was going to have to up the stakes." He looked at Floyd and gave a self-conscious smile. "I tell everybody. I wouldn't be here today if it weren't for you."

Floyd wanted to speak but could think of nothing to say.

"Funny, isn't it?" Barrington went on. "It was, without question, the worst day of my life, but that's when it all really started. That's when I began to *work*. That's when I decided where I really wanted to go." He took a sip of his drink. "Mind you, I'd have done it a lot quicker if I'd had someone like your father looking after me." He looked carefully at Floyd. "You know I asked him?"

"Asked him what?"

"To be my coach. It was about a month after the match and I thought, if it was true that you'd dropped out, then there was one very good coach in need of a student. So I called your dad and asked if he'd take me on."

"What did he say?"

"He said no. But he was very polite. And he gave me the name of someone in America he said I should contact if I was serious. So I did."

"Daniel Rowse . . ." Floyd nodded.

"Right. Your dad put in a good word for me, so that's where I went. And it seems to have worked out OK."

Floyd looked at Barrington, sitting back in his chair in the tennis world's holy of holies, looking completely at ease and at home. Tomorrow he would be going out on Centre Court to play the number one seed in the quarterfinals of the most prestigious tennis tournament in the world and . . . yes, you could say it seemed to have worked out OK.

"Have you ever thought about coming back?" asked Barrington.

"What?"

"It wouldn't be too late. Plenty of people dip out for a couple of years with injuries, and in twelve months they're right back up where they were. You could do it."

"I don't think so," said Floyd.

"Are you sure?" Barrington gestured to the room around them. "You don't ever wonder if you made the wrong choice, giving up . . . all this?"

"It wasn't really a choice," said Floyd. "There was a part of me that just didn't want to play tennis." He glanced up at one of the television screens. "Alice has lost. I'd better get back."

"Yeah. And I have to do my little show." Barrington stood up. "I'll walk you out."

"Thanks for the drink," said Floyd. "And good luck tomorrow."

"With Malkowich? I'll need it, won't I?" Barrington chuckled. "But he's not going to get a walk in the park. I'm going to make him work for every single shot. I learned that from you." He smiled. "But if I do lose, it means I'll have time to come and see this aquarium of yours and you can tell me what's so wonderful about fish. Deal?"

"OK," said Floyd.

"Good." Barrington led the way to the door. "And if you ever change your mind about tennis . . . I'm not the only one who'd like to see you back."

Floyd was standing on the sidewalk outside the parking lot entrance when his parents appeared with ten-year-old Sissie in tow.

"Sorry we're late," said his father. "Match was delayed by rain."

"I heard," said Floyd. He had decided not to mention his meeting with Barrington. "Was it a good game?"

"It was incredible!" Sissie was clearly on a high. "Did you know Alice Webber is only seventeen? Can you believe it? Getting to the quarterfinals of Wimbledon when you're only seventeen?"

As they walked to the car, Floyd listened as Sissie told him, in great detail, about both of the matches she had seen, of the mood of the crowd, of the celebrities who had been there, of the astonishing speed of play . . . As they climbed into the car, she started talking about Barrington Gates, and asked Floyd's father if he thought there was a chance of his winning the next day against Malkowich, but Mr. Beresford didn't answer that one and she went back to talking about what they had had for lunch.

Listening to her excited chatter, Floyd remembered how it had been on his own initial visit to Wimbledon—his first sight of the lawns and the stands, the men in blazers and white hats, the women in their brightest dresses, and the buzz that ran through the crowd when the players emerged from the locker room. It was thrilling enough for anyone who enjoyed tennis, but the excitement was quadrupled if, as Sissie did, you had the dream that one day you might be one of the players to come striding out onto the court. A dream, Floyd remembered, that he had once had himself.

As they drove home, he couldn't help thinking about what Barrington had said. He thought of Barrington's car and his clothes. He thought of the girls who had gathered around him at the entrance asking for an autograph, and he thought of the cheers that would go up tomorrow when he came out to challenge the number one seed on Centre Court.

Barrington was right. It *was* a lot to have given up.

And there came, sneaking into his mind, the thought that Barrington might also have been right when he said it wasn't too late. Maybe he *could* choose to play again. A few years out of the game didn't have to mean the end of a career. Some of the greatest tennis players in the world had taken a year out to recover from illness or injury. Sure, it would take him a while to get back to form—he'd have to get fit, train, put in the hours—and of course he'd have to start again at the bottom. Play in the lower league tournaments to build up points and work his way up the rankings. But he could do it. He knew he could, if only . . .

The car drew up at some traffic lights and Floyd glanced out of the window to see a familiar figure standing outside the entrance to a large block of offices. It was Mike. He was looking straight at Floyd, and there was a look of horror on his face that said, as clearly as any words, *What are you thinking!*

Shaking his head in weary disbelief, Mike turned around and began banging his head against the wall of the building. It looked painful, but he didn't stop. He was still banging his head against the brickwork as the lights changed and the car moved off, though he did take one hand out of his pocket to wave good-bye.

Floyd smiled.

It was the only time he ever thought seriously of going back to tennis.

One of Dr. Pinner's theories—he had several—was that, with Mike, Floyd had somehow opened a door to a part of his mind that most of us are rarely able to reach. Mike might have started out as the simple projection of an unconscious desire, he argued, but he had since become a means by which Floyd could access other parts of his unconscious, including that part that holds the deepest intuitive knowledge of who we are and what we should be doing.

To believe that, of course, you had to believe that there *was* a part of the mind that held a deep intuitive knowledge, and, despite all that had happened, Floyd was never too sure about that himself. However, he had a long-standing promise to tell the psychologist if Mike ever reappeared, so he sat down that evening and wrote him an email describing what had happened. He was not entirely surprised to get a reply an hour later asking if Floyd might be free to meet at the Sheridan the next day.

Over their usual tea and cake, the psychologist made Floyd go over everything that had happened and, in particular, everything that Mike had done.

"It was Barrington that Mike wanted you to meet," said Dr. Pinner. "That's the key. And if Mike wanted you to meet Barrington, it must be because there was something you needed to hear from him. You're sure all he talked about was the past? He didn't have any advice for you—any suggestions for the future?"

"You mean apart from saying that it wasn't too late for me to get back into tennis?" asked Floyd. "No. Nothing I can think of, anyway."

But later that evening, on Dr. Pinner's advice, he actually sat down and tried to write down as much as he could remember of the conversation he had had with Barrington Gates in the Members' Bar at Wimbledon.

It left him none the wiser.

• • •

Two days after the trip to London, Barrington appeared at Waterworld. How exactly he had found the place, Floyd never knew, though there were probably not that many aquariums in Sheffield. It was the middle of the afternoon, and Floyd was busily cleaning off the marks of sticky fingers and runny noses from the glass front of one of the tanks when he looked up to find Barrington, spinning a pair of sunglasses in his fingers and smiling amiably down.

"Hi," he said. "I lost yesterday, so . . . here I am."

Barrington had indeed lost his quarterfinal against Malkowich, but only just. The match had been closer than anyone had expected. It went to five sets, with three tiebreakers, and the crowd had gone wild. Television coverage had been huge and Barrington, despite losing, was a new British hero.

"You played well, though," said Floyd. "Everyone said. You played very well." He had watched the highlights of the match on the television in his bedroom, and supper with his parents that evening had been a particularly subdued affair.

"I made him work for it, didn't I?" Barrington looked up and down at the tanks that lined the corridor. "OK . . . are you going to show me around?"

Floyd gave him the Waterworld tour. While rattling off the names and types of fish on display, he told him some of the stories and details of how they had been acquired. He showed him the electric eel, and then did his trick of putting an octopus on his fist before peeling it off, and

Barrington watched and listened politely through it all, though with a slightly bemused expression on his face.

"I hope you won't be offended," he said as Floyd finally led him upstairs to the coffee bar. "I mean, it's all very interesting and you're a great guide, but I still don't quite get it. You actually gave up tennis for . . . for this?"

"Well . . ." Floyd hesitated. "Yes, I suppose I did."

"Why?" Barrington was genuinely puzzled. "I mean . . . they're *fish*!"

Floyd did his best to explain. He told Barrington how he could still remember that first time he had walked into a pet shop when he was five and been mesmerized by the sight of the creatures swimming around in the tanks. How he had been instantly drawn to them, wanting to know more about them and the world in which they lived. How that desire had grown over the years, how he had read and studied, and even collected, a growing number of specimens for himself.

Barrington listened in silence as he sipped his coffee. "So this is it?" he asked, when Floyd had finished. "This is where you're going to be working the rest of your life?"

"No, I don't think so," said Floyd. "I mean, I could if I wanted, but . . . no." He paused and then, in an effort as much as anything to give the impression that his life was not entirely devoid of opportunity, added, "I've had an offer to go to America."

"To do what?"

"I know someone who's doing this research trip in the Gulf of Mexico. On the causes of hypoxia. That's when the oxygen level in the water goes down and the fish start dying. He's trying to find out why."

"Great. When are you going?"

"Well, it's not definite or anything. I can only go if I get scuba diving qualifications. Then I'd have to get a visa. It's quite complicated."

"Complicated?" Barrington stared at him. "Are you kidding? Complicated is training six hours a day for ten years to be a professional tennis player. Learning to scuba dive and getting a visa is something people do every year just to go on vacation." He looked at Floyd. "How come you were offered this job, anyway? Because of the work you do here?"

"Not exactly." Floyd found himself blushing slightly. "The man organizing the trip is the father of this girl I met a few years back. I think she suggested it. I'm not sure why."

"I give up"—Barrington leaned back in his chair— "I really do. A girl asks her father to give you a job, and you don't know why?" He pointed a finger at Floyd's chest. "You get on and do it, OK? Because if you don't, I'm coming back here and I'm going to buy your favorite octopus and eat it."

At that point one of a group of girls who had been hovering at a nearby table stepped forward and asked Barrington if he really was Barrington Gates because she'd watched the match the day before and thought he was *so* wonderful and could she please have an autograph?

Floyd went over to the machine to get another coffee and, while he was there, the Chief appeared beside him and pointed to Barrington.

"Is that him?" he murmured. "The tennis guy?"

Floyd agreed that it was.

"He a friend of yours?"

"I'm not sure he's a friend, exactly," said Floyd. "I played tennis against him once."

"Did you . . . ?" The Chief looked across at Barrington, surrounded by giggling girls. "No shame in losing that one, eh?"

"As a matter of fact," said Floyd, "when I played him, I won."

The Chief gave one of his rare smiles. "Yeah. 'Course you did!"

• • •

That evening, Floyd wrote to Dr. Lamont saying that he had signed up for a scuba diving course, that he had written to the U.S. embassy to apply for a visa, and that he would very much like to accept the offer of a place on his marine research trip the following January.

A slight blip arose in Floyd's plans when, in early September, his job at Waterworld—which he had presumed would be there for as long as he wanted—suddenly came to an end.

It was one of those times when a severe dip in the national economy had hit a good many businesses—even Floyd's parents had been muttering about falling orders and having to cut back to weather the storm—and the news that the Chief no longer had the funds to support a loss-making aquarium was not entirely a surprise.

The Chief himself was in the hospital at the time, recovering from a heart bypass operation, and it was the

Chief's wife who gave Floyd the news. She told him that, sadly, there was no choice but to close Waterworld and that she hoped Floyd would stay on for a couple of weeks to help relocate or sell the stock that had been so carefully acquired over the last three years.

Two weeks later, finding himself without work but still with diving lessons and his flight to America to pay for, Floyd found that the same dip in the economy that had forced Waterworld to close made even the lowest paid part-time work difficult to find. It was in a mood of deep discouragement that, after a morning spent delivering copies of his résumé to hotels, restaurants, and shops without receiving a flicker of interest, he was walking back to the bus station when he saw Mike sitting on a bench in Leopold Square.

He beckoned Floyd to come over and join him.

"I don't suppose," said Floyd, speaking out of the side of his mouth in the hope that no one would notice, "that you're here with a suggestion about what I can do to earn some money?"

Mike smiled but did not answer.

"Only I could use some help on this one," said Floyd. "If I'm going to get to America, I need to—"

"You should talk," interrupted Mike, "to Mrs. Drickett."

"Who?"

"Mrs. Drickett," Mike repeated.

It was still several seconds before Floyd realized who he meant.

"Sandra's mother?" It had been some time since his brief relationship with Sandra, and Floyd had not seen her, or her mother, for at least a year. "Why?"

"She works at the Job Center now."

"I've already tried the Job Center," said Floyd. "They don't have anything. Not for people like me. If I was an IT expert or a bricklayer . . ."

"Floyd?"

Floyd looked up to find an attractively dressed middle-aged woman gazing down at him, a look of concern on her face.

He recognized her at once.

"I don't mean to disturb you," said the woman, "but I was a little worried. You seemed to be talking to yourself. Is everything OK?"

"It's very kind of you to ask, Mrs. Drickett." Floyd glanced to the side and was not surprised to see that Mike had vanished. "But no . . . No, everything's not OK, really. I've been trying to find a job and I'm not having much luck."

"A job?" Mrs. Drickett sat down on the bench beside him. "What sort of job?"

"Anything, really. I just need to earn some money to go to America next year. I've tried everywhere. Today I've been handing out these . . ." He held out the sheaf of copies of his résumé. "But no one's interested."

"Could I see that?" Mrs. Drickett reached across for a copy of his résumé and started reading. "I work at the Job Center these days and there's quite an art to writing a good résumé. I always tell people . . ." She paused. "It doesn't say anything here about your tennis. Is there a reason for that?"

"I don't play tennis anymore," said Floyd.

"I know you don't play competitively, but it's a skill you could use in other ways, isn't it? Like coaching or something? With your reputation, I'd have thought they'd be lining up for that." Mrs. Drickett gave a shrug. "Still, if you're not interested . . ."

She went back to studying the résumé.

"If I *was* interested," said Floyd slowly, "in coaching tennis, how exactly would I go about getting that sort of work?"

"Your dad would be the one to answer that, I think," said Mrs. Drickett. "He knows pretty much everyone in the tennis world, doesn't he?"

• • •

That evening, a little hesitantly, Floyd asked his father if he thought there was any chance of his getting work as a tennis coach and was relieved to find that Mr. Beresford did not seem to be upset at the suggestion. He listened carefully while Floyd explained what Sandra's mother had told him, nodded, and said that he would ask around.

Two days later he took Floyd to a small private school four miles outside Sheffield that needed a temporary replacement for a gym coach who had gone on maternity leave. The headmaster, a grizzled-looking man in his fifties, took Floyd down to the courts—which Floyd's father had built—and asked him to start coaching a twelve-year-old boy who was already standing there, waiting.

Floyd had not expected things to happen so fast and was not exactly prepared. He had not touched a tennis racket for over three years and wasn't at all sure he could still make the ball do anything if he did, let alone teach the principles to anyone else. Putting these worries aside, however, he began by getting the boy to do the sort of warm-up exercises that his father had done with him every day for ten years and found, as he did so, that he fell almost automatically into his father's easy and encouraging style. He did his best to keep it fun, to explain one thing, practice it, then move on to something different before his pupil had time to get bored . . . From the start, the whole thing felt remarkably natural and easy.

Fifteen minutes later, the headmaster came across to tell the boy, whose name was Freddie Stripes, that it was time he got back to his class. Then he turned to Floyd.

"So when can you start?"

"Well . . . any time, really," said Floyd.

The headmaster looked at his watch. "If I gave you six children, the same age as Freddie, could you look after them for an hour?"

"What, now?"

"Yes. There'll be a member of the staff down here with you in case you have any problems. But I can see you won't."

"OK. Yes. Yes, that's fine."

"Good." The headmaster was already turning to leave. "Your dad says he'll be back to pick you up after lunch."

Dr. Pinner laughed when he heard. "I told you there was no need to worry," he said.

• • •

Floyd enjoyed the coaching. Most of the time it hardly felt like work at all, and it reminded him of all the things he had enjoyed about tennis while he was growing up—the being outdoors, the pleasure of physical exertion, the satisfaction brought by acquiring a new skill. And the job not only paid three times what he had been earning at Waterworld, it also quite unexpectedly began to heal the rift that had opened between Floyd and his parents after Roehampton.

It did so firstly because, in teaching others, Floyd came to appreciate how good his parents, and particularly his father, had been at teaching him. It seemed only natural that he should start asking his father's advice when it came to planning lessons or talking about why something hadn't worked the way he had hoped and asking how he could do it better. At supper his parents would want to know how his day had gone and, for the first time in years, the evening meal became what it had been for so much of his life—a time when they all came together to discuss what had happened during the day and to share their plans for the next.

But there was one other equally unexpected offshoot from the coaching job. For most of the boys Floyd taught, tennis was a sport they chose because it was fun. Some of them were good athletes, and the tennis team next year would be a strong one, but for one of the boys the game was clearly something more.

Floyd had noticed the difference that first day. Freddie Stripes wasn't just a keen player—there was a *hunger* about him. He was always early for practice, seemed to eat up any coaching, and was to be found on one of the courts at any spare moment he had during the day. It was toward the end of the semester, after a class, that Floyd found Freddie's mother waiting outside the gym when he had finished.

"Mr. Beresford?" she said. "Could I have a word?"

"Yes, of course." Floyd was beginning to get used to people calling him "Mr. Beresford."

"Freddie has very much enjoyed his lessons with you," said Mrs. Stripes, "and he's been asking if we could organize some extra instruction for him."

"Sounds like a good idea," said Floyd. "He's an excellent player."

"Thank you. We wondered if *you* would be prepared to coach him. On weekends, perhaps? Or early mornings? We would pay you, of course."

"I'm sorry," said Floyd, "but I'm only here for this semester. After Christmas, I'm going to America."

"Ah . . . Freddie will be disappointed to hear that." Mrs. Stripes paused briefly before continuing. "But I think he needs someone, don't you? I mean, it seems to us he has a lot of talent."

"I agree," said Floyd. "He does."

"So who would be the best person to teach him, do you think? Is there anyone you could recommend?"

Floyd thought about this.

"I don't know if you can get him," he said eventually, "but the best person would be my father."

Three weeks later, Floyd found himself standing on a dockside on Jeffries Point in Boston, looking up at the ship that was to be his home for the next three months. The name on her bow said she was the *We're Here* and, despite his jet lag, the sight of her triggered in Floyd the curious sensation that he had somehow arrived at exactly the place he was supposed to be.

As if to confirm that feeling, he became aware that Mike was standing beside him, with a smile on his face very similar to the one he had had that first day on the beach at Bude, sitting on a rock and looking out to sea. He even made the same admiring gesture with his arm that seemed to say, *Isn't that fantastic!*

"She's beautiful," said Floyd. "Really beautiful!"

"Glad you like her," said a voice. "Kind of fond of her myself."

Floyd turned to find that the figure beside him was not Mike, but a young man with straggly hair trailing several inches over his collar and a beard carefully woven into three plaits.

"Name's Gosta," said the man. "I'm one of the scientists."

"I'm Floyd," said Floyd. "I think I'm the gofer."

Gosta grinned, put a hand on Floyd's shoulder, and led him toward the gangway.

"Come on," he said. "I'll show you around."

• • •

The *We're Here* was a vessel of some two hundred tons, with a crew of four and accommodations for six scientists. Officially, Floyd was on the books as a scientist but, as is often the case on small boats, the difference between the two categories was fluid. Three of the scientists were also licensed to keep watch, while all of the "crew" were experienced divers, and Floyd was as frequently asked to take a turn at watchkeeping as he was to help dive for the samples and specimens that were being collected. The reason he looked as if he was enjoying himself doing either was because he was.

Much of the work he did as a member of the crew involved, as Dr. Lamont had warned, doing whatever anyone asked him to, but he didn't seem to mind. Whether he was being a "wiper" down in the engine room, a cook in the galley, or standing watch at night, Floyd always gave the impression that he was not only happy doing whatever it was, but thriving on it.

The work he did for the scientists was mentally more demanding, but he thrived on that as well. Part of the research involved recording which species of fish were still surviving in the oxygen-depleted waters, and Floyd found that, in this area, his value was much more than that of a gofer. Three years working in an aquarium in Sheffield had given him an easy familiarity with most of the species they encountered and a confidence in identifying them that was at least the equal of anyone else on board. As a result, he was asked to do a good deal of diving. Which he loved.

His diving partner was usually Gosta, a man everyone referred to as "the Bear," because of the remarkable quantity of hair that covered his body. Gosta talked a good deal about the environmental doom that he was convinced would shortly overtake the planet, in distinct contrast to Floyd's more optimistic outlook, but for some reason the two of them rapidly became friends.

And it was the people on the *We're Here* that Floyd loved best. The hypoxic "dead zone" in the Gulf of Mexico is the second biggest in the world, and the most probable cause is the amount of fertilizer used on farms along the Mississippi that gets washed into the river and then down to the sea. Dr. Lamont's research was aimed at determining which levels were the most dangerous and how the damage could be reversed. There was nowhere he would rather be, Floyd thought, than with the people who could analyze such problems and work out a possible solution.

Most of them were considerably older than he was, but they were all interested in the same things, they all wanted to achieve the same results, and they all had the same concerns. Floyd found that being with them, listening to their stories, hearing them argue, and asking them questions, gave him the feeling for the first time in his life that he had found a place within his own tribe. As he later said, the moment he stepped on board, he did not simply feel *at* home, he felt that he had *come* home.

• • •

At the end of the commission, the *We're Here* returned to Boston, and Dr. Lamont invited Floyd to stay at his house on the university grounds for a few days before flying back to England. Charity was there, fresh from her second semester at Cornell, and she took him, as she had promised, on several trips to see the sights of Boston. The first of these was in a dinghy, which the Lamonts kept at Rowes Wharf, to see the views from the waterfront.

Sitting in the little boat while Charity steered it skillfully through the other traffic on the water, Floyd found himself less interested in the view than in telling Charity about his time in the Gulf of Mexico. He described the extraordinary diversity of marine life he had seen there, told her about his admiration for the crew of the *We're Here* and his friendship with Gosta, and then about that curious feeling he had had of "coming home," and being with his own tribe.

And Charity listened, in the same way she had listened on the beach at Holacombe in Cornwall, without interruption.

"So what do you do now?" she asked when he had finished.

"Well, your dad's invited me to come on the next trip he's doing—to the Caribbean."

"That's good," said Charity.

"But it's not till the summer. So I thought, between now and then, I'd try and get some qualifications. Maybe a watchkeeping certificate, learn some navigation . . ."

"So that one day you could join as part of the crew?"

Floyd nodded. "That's the plan. I think it's the sort of job that would suit me."

"Yes . . ." Charity frowned.

"What is it? What's wrong?"

"Well, I just thought . . ." Charity tightened a sheet and steered them around a party of children in kayaks. "From the way you talk, it's obvious how much you enjoyed doing all the science stuff, as well. And Dad says you were really good at it. Couldn't you do that too?"

"I'd need to have done university before I could do any real work on the science side," said Floyd.

"Yes," Charity agreed. "I suppose you would."

"And I'd have had to apply months ago if I was going to do that. I've kind of missed the boat on that one."

"Have you?" said Charity. "That's a shame."

• • •

Her parents, when the subject came up at supper that evening, agreed that it was indeed a shame and, when the meal ended, Dr. Lamont got up from the table and disappeared into his office. He came back half an hour later with the news that he had been talking to his friend Dr. McKinley, who ran what was probably the best marine biology course in the U.K. at the University of Exeter. When Floyd returned to England, he said, there would be a place for him if he wanted, starting in September.

In early July, Floyd flew back to Boston to join the *We're Here* as she set off to spend eight weeks investigating the decline of reef-building corals on the Mouchoir Bank in the Caribbean. And it was there, some forty miles to the east of the Turks and Caicos Islands, that he saw Mike for the last and undoubtedly the strangest time.

Dr. Lamont had warned everyone before they sailed that this was possibly going to be their final voyage on the *We're Here*. A large part of the funds that had financed the boat and its research had been provided by a trust set up by a man who had made his fortune in the tuna trade. Unfortunately, that funding would soon be coming to an end and as yet no new sponsor had been found.

It was a disappointment, especially to those members of the team who had worked together for a good number of years and formed strong friendships in the process, but it was, despite that, a particularly happy voyage. For Floyd, there was the added bonus that, to his surprise, Charity had joined the ship as well. It seemed her course at Cornell required that she do a number of weeks of fieldwork, and that two months on the *We're Here* fit perfectly.

It was in their fourth week out that Floyd saw Mike. The *We're Here* was anchored in about sixty feet of water while its divers collected mollusks. The aim was to gather a series of samples from layers excavated on the seafloor, to find out exactly when and how the recent changes to the marine environment had taken place. Floyd and the Bear were diving together that morning, collecting shells from a pit that had been started the previous day, and the Bear was carrying a tray of them up to the boat when it happened.

While the Bear swam to the surface, Floyd had stayed on the seabed, making a start on excavating the next layer of shells. At least that's what he would have done if he hadn't suddenly noticed Mike, standing on the seabed a few yards away. He was dressed exactly as he had been on the tennis court at Roehampton and the street in Wimbledon, and had the same thoughtful look on his face as he gave his usual nod of greeting.

Almost instinctively, Floyd put down his trowel and began moving toward the figure. As he did so, Mike lifted an arm, pointed to somewhere over on his right, and then began walking in that direction, beckoning Floyd to follow.

It is a golden rule of diving safety that you always do everything in pairs. Diving on your own, without someone to help if you get into difficulty, is how accidents happen. Strictly speaking, Floyd staying on the seabed even for the minute or so it took the Bear to take a tray of specimens to the surface and come back was already stretching the rules. Swimming off somewhere without telling your diving partner where you were going was . . . unthinkable.

But for some reason Floyd did *not* think about it. Mike was beckoning him to follow, and he did not hesitate to do exactly that. His friend was walking at a pace that required Floyd to swim at full stretch to keep up, and although he wondered where they might be going and why, he still followed. He followed, even when the regulator on his wrist told him that the tank of air on his back was now using its safety reserve. Ignoring the warning, he just kept following while Mike kept beckoning him on.

He had been swimming for almost twenty minutes when Mike finally came to a halt in an area of seabed where the sand was littered with coral outcrops, rocks, and undulating seaweed. Calmly seating himself on a large section of coral, he pointed to something beside him. Floyd swam over to investigate. Looking closely, he saw that Mike was pointing at something wedged in a crevice, and when he reached down and took it out, he found it was a small metal button.

That's it? Floyd thought. This is why you made me follow you? So you could show me a button?

Mike smiled, then pointed upward. Glancing at the gauge on his wrist, Floyd realized he had only a few minutes of air left—and then felt Mike's hand on his elbow, pushing him, physically pushing him, directly up toward the surface.

It was only as he took his first breath of fresh air that Floyd realized how bizarre his behavior was going to look to the others on the boat. Indeed, how bizarre it had actually been. Mike had disappeared somewhere on the journey to the surface and, when he scanned the horizon, Floyd could see no sign of the *We're Here*. He wasn't even sure precisely in which direction it lay, so trying to swim back to it was probably not the best method. With a sigh, he switched on the little radio beacon Dr. Lamont made all the divers carry, which would send a signal indicating where he was so that they could come and pick him up.

After that, there was nothing to do but wait. It could, he reckoned, be a while before anyone noticed the signal, then it would take perhaps another ten minutes to winch up the anchor and get under way, and the same time again to cover the mile or so to pick him up. Dr. Lamont wouldn't waste diesel traveling at anything faster than eight or nine knots, so he probably had about half an hour before they came to retrieve him. Half an hour in which to try to think how on earth he was going to explain his behavior—and try *not* to think of how angry Dr. Lamont was going to be when he appeared.

He was wrong about the timing. It was barely a minute before the white hull of the *We're Here* was visible on the horizon, its bow ploughing through the water at a distinctly uneconomic speed, and only a few minutes more before it hove to alongside, with most of the crew peering anxiously down over the rail.

"Throw him a line," called Dr. Lamont. "Let's get him in! Fast as you can!" He looked down at Floyd. "Are you all right?"

"I'm fine!" shouted Floyd.

Someone threw him a rope and he was hauled toward the stern of the boat where a dozen hands were eagerly waiting to help pull him aboard.

"Easy now . . . Give him room to breathe . . . You're sure you're OK? Sit him down over here . . ."

More pairs of hands were unstrapping his tank and removing his mask and peeling back his wetsuit. It was not quite the angry reception Floyd had been expecting.

"You're not hurt or anything? Really? You're all right?"

That was Charity, her face white and worried only a few inches from his own, looking as if she had recently been crying.

"Here, drink this . . ." The Bear was thrusting a glass of brandy into Floyd's hand. "By God but you had us worried!"

Floyd was too embarrassed to speak. How could he have been so stupid? Of course they were worried. A team member disappears underwater without a trace for more than twenty minutes—what else could they be but worried? And they all thought there must be a reasonable explanation. How was he going to tell them that he'd caused all this panic because he had been following an invisible friend?

"I'm sorry if I worried you all, I . . . I . . ." He searched for the words that would explain convincingly about Mike and realized there weren't any. "I decided to go for a swim," he finished lamely.

"I told you!" That was the Bear again. "I told you he wouldn't just sit there!"

"It was risky." Dr. Lamont was smiling down at him. "But you did the right thing. It's still out there, circling the site. You'd never have got up if you hadn't moved."

"I told you he'd swim for it!" The Bear beamed around triumphantly, his plaited beard shaking with pleasure. "I told you! He's smart, this one!"

16

It was a while before Floyd pieced together the story of what had happened on the surface while he had been busy following Mike on the seabed.

It had started when the Bear had swum back up to the boat with the tray of mollusks. He had passed it to Natalie, who was manning the safety rope, and was about to dive back down when he saw the shark.

Marine biologists are not, as a rule, bothered by the sight of a shark. If anything, their natural inclination is to swim toward it for a closer look. This particular shark, however—it was a large adult *Isurus*—was, the Bear noted, heading straight at him with a speed and a sense of purpose that made him decide to get out of the water. Fast.

Normally, a diver climbing out of the water onto the boat had to first remove his fins, so that his feet would fit on the ladder hanging over the stern. Then, halfway up the ladder he would pause to remove his mask, take the breather out of his mouth, and unclip the weights from around his waist before finally heaving himself back on board.

With the shark bearing down on him, the Bear did none of those things. He simply hauled himself upward using the strength of his arms, and just managed to lift himself clear of the water as the shark, its mouth gaping open to reveal an impressive array of teeth, swept past inches beneath him. As Natalie helped heave the Bear into the boat, it was already turning to come in for another attack.

An *Isurus*, or mako shark, is one of the very few species that will attack humans, and they can swim at an astonishing pace. They have been known to reach speeds on an attack run of sixty miles an hour, and adults like this one can be up to twelve feet long and weigh the better part of half a ton. It makes them, if they do decide to attack, a formidable threat.

Natalie's shouts had brought most of the rest of the crew to the stern of the boat from where, as she and the Bear explained the situation, the shark was still visible. It was swimming in a circle around the *We're Here*, just below the surface, at a distance of about ten yards. While everyone was relieved that the Bear had been pulled to safety, the real concern was for Floyd. As Natalie pointed out, if he tried to come up while the shark was still circling and it behaved as aggressively toward him as it had toward the Bear, then he could be in serious danger.

"When's he due?" asked Dr. Lamont.

"Not for seven . . . eight minutes." The Bear looked at his watch. "But he's going to start wondering where I am soon, isn't he . . . ? He could come up at any time to find out what's happened."

"Someone needs to tell him to stay down there," said Charity, "until it's safe."

"We'll lower a message board," said Dr. Lamont. "And a spare tank of air in case he has to stay down a bit longer." He paused. "And I want someone to get back in the water. We need to know if that shark goes for anyone, or if it was just the Bear it didn't like."

An Australian crew member called Warren volunteered to test the water. He was already suited up, ready to take over as part of the next shift, but had got no more than half a leg in the water before the warning shout came that the shark had turned and was racing toward him.

It raced with equal speed toward the message board and the spare air tank that they lowered over the side but, after a brief investigation, ignored them and went back to circling the boat. The message board warned Floyd about the shark and told him to stay on the seabed until he got word it was safe, but there was, worryingly, no indication that he had read it. If he had, surely he would have signaled the fact by giving a tug on the rope?

The alarming possibility was that Floyd, last seen cheerily digging on the seabed with a little cloud of sediment obscuring his view of the events around him, might still have no idea what was going on sixty feet above him. With low cloud cover, visibility underwater that day was not good, and unless he had been looking in the right direction, there was no guarantee that he had even seen the spare air tank they had lowered or read the message that was tied to it. Any minute now, still happily unaware of the danger, he might decide to return to the surface to find himself at the mercy of an extremely aggressive *Isurus*.

Someone had already been dispatched to bring up the rifle that was stored in one of the rope lockers, and Dr. Lamont had detailed two of his scientists to haul out the shark cage from its storage space in the bow. In a pinch, he thought, they would be able either to kill the shark or send down someone in the cage to rescue Floyd.

Several minutes later, the crew member detailed to get the rifle returned with the news that, although he had found the gun, the key to the steel ammunition cupboard seemed to be missing. The crew members dispatched for the shark cage had had better luck and were soon to be seen assembling it on deck, but this was, as everyone knew, a task that could take anywhere up to an hour.

And the shark was still circling. Every few minutes, someone on the team would try to slip quietly into the water, but the result was always the same—an instant and astonishingly fast attack. By now, the worry was that Floyd had *not* come up. It was several minutes past the time when his regulator should have told him to come to the surface, but there was no indication of why he had not come up or why he had decided to stay on the seafloor. He had not used the safety rope to signal he was in difficulty. There was no indication that he had found the spare tank of air with its attached message, and although he probably still had another ten or fifteen minutes of air, this lack of communication was the most worrying thing of all.

"I think he swam away," said the Bear. "He saw the shark, and he swam away."

It was an encouraging thought if it was true, but the Bear seemed to be the only one who believed it.

Eventually, and in sheer desperation, Dr. Lamont and the captain gave orders to slip the anchor and sail north. The mako shark's aggression toward humans is believed to be because it sees them as rivals for its food supply and is attempting to drive them away. If they moved, Dr. Lamont reasoned, maybe the shark would go with them, herding them out of its territory so that when Floyd did come to the surface the shark would no longer be there.

Nor would anyone else of course, and the idea of leaving Floyd behind, even with an inflatable dinghy ready for him to climb into when he surfaced, did not sit well with some of the crew. But there was no time for debate. No time even to raise the anchor, which was simply abandoned as the *We're Here* cut the cable and headed north.

It was a difficult decision to have made, and even worse was the news that it had not worked. The shark was being tracked on radar by Warren in the wheelhouse, and he reported that not only had it failed to follow them but it seemed to have gone deep. It was no longer swimming near the surface, but down on the seabed circling precisely the area where Floyd and the Bear had been digging.

A black silence descended on the crew when they received this news, though the Bear was still insisting that he thought Floyd would have swum away.

"He's smart, that boy," he muttered to an ashen-faced Charity. "I'm telling you, he already swam away. Early on. He swam away!"

His face a grim mask, Dr. Lamont had just given orders for the boat to return to the diving site when a shout from Warren said he was picking up a signal from Floyd's radio transmitter, a mile and a half to the east. Within seconds, the *We're Here* had turned and was heading in its direction with every ounce of power that her EMD diesel engines could provide.

. . .

The story came out in bits, with everyone chipping in their own comments and contributions—everyone that is, except Charity. She sat beside Floyd on the bench, not saying anything, but with her body pressed firmly against his and holding one of his hands tightly in her own.

Dr. Lamont told her to take Floyd below and check that he was all right—she was the one with the most recent first aid training—but once belowdecks, instead of checking his condition, she simply wrapped her arms around him and burst into tears.

When Floyd asked what the matter was, she responded by kissing him with some passion while still crying, only breaking off occasionally to say between sobs, "I thought you were gone. I thought I'd lost you. I couldn't bear it if I lost you . . ."

Floyd, in between kissing her back, assured her that there was no way she was ever going to lose him, and in the following hour said a good many other things besides.

When the two of them eventually reappeared on deck, it was to find the *We're Here* back at her diving site, with the Bear sitting up in the bow with a rifle—the key to the ammunition locker had eventually been found—and the news that the shark seemed to have vanished as mysteriously as it had arrived.

"Not a trace of it anywhere!" said Dr. Lamont cheerfully, walking briskly across the deck toward them. He looked carefully at Floyd, and then at his daughter. "So how's the patient?"

"He's all right," said Charity. "In fact . . . he's very all right."

"Is he?" Her father looked thoughtfully at Floyd, and then his gaze traveled down to where Charity was still firmly holding Floyd's hand.

"Good," he said, his mouth twitching into a smile. "I'm glad to hear it."

And he set off back to the stern of the boat, where Natalie was attempting to organize lowering the shark cage into the water.

• • •

That night, Floyd and the Bear had the middle watch—the four hours after midnight—and the two of them sat on the benches set into the bulwarks of the bow of the *We're Here* and talked. They talked about what had happened that day and about how easily it could all have turned out so differently, and then Floyd talked about the miracle he was still trying to absorb, of discovering that not only was he in love but that the girl in question felt the same way about him.

"I suppose, in a way, I ought to be grateful to that shark," he said. "If it hadn't turned up when it did, Charity might never have realized how she felt about me."

The Bear looked at him, a puzzled frown on his face.

"It was thinking that I might have died or something," Floyd explained, "that made her realize that she . . . that she cared about me. Before today, she hadn't the least idea."

The Bear was still frowning. "She told you that?"

Floyd nodded. "It's weird, isn't it?" He leaned back and looked up at the stars hanging bright and clear in the night sky. "I mean, we've always *liked* each other, and we had this sort of thing when we were fifteen, but . . ."

"But you didn't know?"

"No. Neither of us did!"

The Bear let out a long sigh.

"And there's me been telling everyone how smart you are," he muttered.

PART

1

In a sense, that is where this story rightfully comes to an end. It is, after all, the story of Mike, and that occasion on the Mouchoir Bank was the last time that Floyd saw him. Since the day Mike led him to safety, striding across the seabed and beckoning him to follow, Floyd has not seen so much as a glimpse of the friend who, over the years, played such a decisive role in his life. Dr. Pinner still writes now and then to ask if there has been another appearance, but the answer is always the same. Like the mako shark on that fateful day, Mike seems to have vanished as suddenly and completely as he first appeared.

But there are, perhaps, a few more things to add before this story is properly complete. Not least is the fact that, if you talk to Charity, she will tell you that Mike did in fact make one more appearance that was, in its way, every bit as remarkable as any of the others.

And before that, of course, there was all the business with the button.

• • •

It was Dr. Pinner who suggested it might be a good idea to take a closer look at the button. Floyd had sent an email to the psychologist the next day, detailing his latest encounter with Mike and asking if he had an explanation for how an imaginary friend could appear in sixty feet of water and lead you to safety from a shark that you did not even know was there.

In his reply, Dr. Pinner said he wondered if the whole thing might not have been the result of some unconscious recognition of danger, rather in the way, he said, that animals were known to flee before an earthquake or a fire. Perhaps some part of Floyd's mind had registered the danger signals even before he was consciously aware of them and "produced" Mike as the quickest and most convincing means of telling him that, to be safe, he needed to be somewhere else. It was only an idea, he added. The truth was that he found it every bit as mysterious as Floyd had.

But he did say, at the end of his email, that he thought it might be worthwhile giving the button to which Mike had led him some close examination.

It's possible, that it's no more than an interesting memento of an extraordinary day, but in all your previous encounters with Mike, almost everything he has said and done has turned out to have some wider significance. I think it might be worth getting someone to look at the button, particularly if it has some symbol on it. It may be that there is an additional message to be found there.

"Button?" said Charity, when Floyd showed her the email. "What button?"

It was the one part of the story that Floyd had not told her—there had been other things on his mind at the time—but he explained now how Mike had pointed to the button in a crevice in the rock just before pushing him up to the surface.

"Have you still got it?" asked Charity and, when Floyd retrieved it from the pocket of his wet suit, examined it carefully.

The only symbol on it that either of them could see was the number sixty with a crown above it, but Charity suggested they show it to Jonas Wilde. Jonas, the ship's engineer, was an enthusiastic historian, and he identified it almost immediately as the coat button from a military uniform.

"Silver," he said confidently. "And British, but give me five minutes and I should be able to tell you more exactly."

He disappeared belowdecks and was back fifteen minutes later with a laptop and a curious smile on his face.

"There you are," he said, pointing to a picture on the screen of a button identical to the one that Floyd had found. "It's from the coat of an officer of the 60th Regiment of the King's Royal Rifle Corps." He paused. "And I can even make a guess at how it got there."

He pressed a key on the computer and the picture of the button was replaced by a page of writing. It was an account of the loss of HMS *Prothea*, a 26-gun frigate on passage from England to Jamaica in 1783 when she had been lost with all hands.

According to the account on the screen, she had been carrying a small detachment of officers for a newly formed battalion of the 60th Regiment, part of the strengthening of the Jamaican defenses in the face of possible French attack. The ship had been hit by a hurricane as she made her way through the Mouchoir Passage to the south of the Turks and Caicos Islands, and sunk. As well as the group of officers, she had been carrying nine hundred and sixty thousand British pounds in gold coins. Much needed pay chests for the troops in Jamaica.

Charity asked Floyd to read that line again.

"Nine hundred and sixty thousand British pounds in gold coins . . ."

"You came straight up to the surface, did you?" asked Jonas casually. "After you found the button?"

"Yes," said Floyd, remembering Mike's hand on his arm, pushing him firmly upward. "Yes, I did."

"So we know exactly where you found this, don't we?" There was a gleam in Jonas's eye. "The location's on the GPS record. There'd be no problem going back."

* * *

Dr. Lamont was not convinced that going back was a good idea. At a meeting in the *We're Here*'s mess hall that night, he pointed out that they had been commissioned to conduct scientific research, not a treasure hunt. Ships wrecked in a hurricane could be scattered over a vast distance and it might take days, weeks, or even months before they found anything of significance. In his view, using a marine research vessel to look for a wrecked treasure ship on the basis of the evidence of a single button simply could not be justified to the trustees who had sponsored them. Some people agreed with him, some did not, and the discussion went back and forth for more than an hour.

"We're not really talking about a treasure hunt, are we?" said Floyd. As the youngest and least qualified member of the crew, he had not spoken before, but slightly to his surprise, everyone stopped to listen. "I mean, I know we don't have the resources for that, but I think we should take a look. Just a quick look, to see what's there." He glanced across the table at Dr. Lamont. "I can't say why exactly, but I think that's what we're supposed to do."

Dr. Lamont did not reply immediately. He sat at the end of the table, thoughtfully tapping a pencil up and down between his fingers.

"Four hours," he said eventually. "I'll give you four hours, and if you haven't found anything by then we get back to work and forget about it, understood?"

In the event, it did not take four hours to establish that they had discovered the location of the wreck of HMS *Prothea*. It took less than four minutes. Floyd and Jonas went down first and, even as they were making their descent, Jonas pointed to the ribbed timbers of what could only be the wreck of a wooden ship, visible to their right. It was heavily encrusted with marine growth, but the cannon scattered in a trail to the east meant it had to have been a warship, and traces of the cargo it had carried were soon visible on the seafloor. One of them was a chest that had conveniently broken open, and a part of its contents—a glistening clump of sovereigns—lay exposed on the sand.

There was another meeting that afternoon in the mess hall of the *We're Here*, and it went on long, long into the evening.

It took two and a half years to get permission to investigate the wreck on the Mouchoir Bank. The government of the Turks and Caicos Islands, in concert with their extremely cautious British advisers—the islands are still a British Overseas Territory—eventually granted a license for Dr. Lamont and his team to search for the wreckage of HMS *Prothea* in a forty-square-mile area of their territorial waters, in return for fifty percent of the value of anything they might find.

In the course of a two-month expedition, gold coins and various other finds with a commercial value of $476 million were brought up from the seabed, and after the expenses of the trip had been paid and the government of the Turks and Caicos given its share, Dr. Lamont and his team found themselves with a fortune of a little over $234 million.

They used the money, as had been agreed at the meeting nearly three years before, to set up a company that would do marine research for governments, universities, or wherever it seemed most needed. Each of the ten members of the crew had equal shares in the company, which they were at liberty to sell if they wished, and a place on the board. It was decided, at the first board meeting, to recommission the *We're Here* so that it could continue its work with Dr. Lamont and Boston University.

Floyd and Charity were married that same year, soon after Floyd had completed his degree and Charity had started work on her PhD. The date of the wedding was carefully timed to avoid any clash with the whale breeding season so that Charity's mother could attend—and was in the week between the French Open and Wimbledon so that Floyd's parents were free to fly over from England. Granny Plum, who had never been on an airplane in her life, was brought over by Dr. Pinner, who kept her calm with industrial-strength doses of valium.

The marriage took place on the university campus, with the ceremony in the beautiful Marsh Chapel and the reception in Boston University Castle. One of the many messages of congratulations that came in was from the

Chief and included the news that Waterworld was back in action, with the offer that, if Floyd ever needed his old job back, he had only to ask. Floyd's favorite card, however, was from Barrington Gates, which said simply, *I still say you could have made more money playing tennis.*

The Bear was Floyd's best man, and in his speech he told the story of how, on the research expedition three years before, it had been pitifully clear to everyone that Charity and Floyd were made for each other, and what a relief it was when the two of them realized this for themselves. The crew, he said, were all extremely grateful to the shark that had finally brought the couple together.

"Is that true?" Floyd asked Charity later. "That everyone knew?"

"Yes," Charity told him. "I think it is."

"But how? How could everyone know, and not us?"

Charity gave a little shrug.

"It's a mystery, isn't it . . . ?" she said, and kissed him.

After Charity had finished her doctorate, she took up a post at the University of South Florida. She and Floyd, who had by then acquired his master's degree, moved down to Tampa, and that was where the main offices of Marine Intel were finally established in a building looking out over Palm Harbor to where the *We're Here* was moored when she was not at sea.

The company has, in the years since then, established a considerable reputation for the quality of its research. Whether you want to know about fish stocks, sea currents, or the effects of climate change, Marine Intel is one of the go-to places that universities and governments know can be trusted to provide accurate and reliable data.

Its three-story offices are on the edge of the Wharf Marina, and Floyd and Charity share a generously large office on the second floor. On one wall hangs a picture, more than three feet wide, of the wreck of the *Prothea*. A barnacled carronade hangs on the opposite wall, and on Floyd's desk, pride of place is given to a silver button set in a large cube of plexiglass.

From the picture window you get a magnificent view out over the water, and that was where Charity was standing to get her first glimpse of the *We're Here II* as she nudged her way toward a berth on the north dock. Floyd's parents were standing beside her, and the three of them stood in silence as they watched the boat slow, then come to a halt as the mooring ropes pulled her into position.

"He did that quite nicely, didn't he?" murmured Mr. Beresford.

"I made him promise not to crash it on the first time out," said Charity. "I wanted you to see it while it was still all shiny and new."

The *We're Here II* had been built in a yard on the Chesapeake. Floyd had taken delivery of her four days before and brought her down to Tampa, which was to be her home port. The plan had been for Charity and Floyd's parents to be waiting on the quayside and then to be given a tour, but it rains sometimes, even in

Florida, so they had watched instead from the company's offices. It was a Saturday, so the building was largely empty.

"He's got to report to the harbormaster first," said Charity. "I suggest we go down after he's done that. The rain might have stopped by then."

"I hadn't realized," said Mrs. Beresford, peering through a pair of binoculars, "it was so big."

"It's going to be a lot more comfortable than the old ship," said Charity happily. "Not quite like a cruise ship, but close! Floyd and I get a double cabin with our own shower!" She turned to her father-in-law. "How's Freddie doing, by the way?"

Freddie Stripes, Mr. Beresford assured her, was doing very well indeed. He had recently become the U.K. number one seed, having toppled Barrington from that position, and Floyd's father was his coach, as he had been for the last six years. In fact, the real reason they had come to the States was that nineteen-year-old Freddie would be playing next week in the Florida Open.

"And he'll win," said Mr. Beresford confidently. "He's going to go all the way is Freddie. All the way..." His voice tailed off. He was watching his son on the deck of the *We're Here II*, checking ropes and fenders before disappearing back for a moment into the wheelhouse. "I know

I shouldn't," he said, with a trace of wistfulness in his voice, "but I still wish sometimes that..." He stopped and looked at Charity. "You never saw him on the court, did you? He was ... such a wonderful player."

Charity took his arm and folded it in her own. "He's a pretty wonderful marine biologist," she said.

On the other side of him, his wife took his other arm. "And he's so happy," she said. "I mean ... look at him!"

And Charity, watching the long, lean figure of her husband emerging from the wheelhouse with his tousled hair and his easy swinging stride, could only agree. Floyd looked very happy. She watched fondly as he clapped one of the crew on the back, called an instruction to another, and then jumped from the deck of the *We're Here II* to the jetty. He gave a wave in the direction of the Marine Intel building, where he knew his wife and parents were watching, then set off along the quay, his ankle-length black oilskins flapping behind him in the wind and rain as he strode toward the harbormaster's office.

And that was when it happened.

Watching him, Charity had a sudden flash of recognition. She had, she knew, seen an almost identical sight somewhere before, though for a moment she could not remember when or where. And then she had it. It was that day on a beach in Cornwall, almost eight years before, when she had seen a figure in a long black coat standing beside Floyd on the sands at Bude.

She smiled to herself at the realization. Floyd, marching along the jetty in his black oilskin coat, looked like Mike.

He looked *exactly* like Mike.

When I said at the beginning that this was a true story, I was perhaps exaggerating a little. Some of it is true, but not all. I had to change the names, obviously, and the bit about Floyd being brilliant at tennis is all made up, as well. So is the part where he meets Charity, then gets a job in an aquarium . . . In fact, none of this story actually happened. Not the way I said it did.

But the bit about Mike is true. Absolutely, one hundred percent. I can say that because I've seen him, heard him (though not as often as I'd like), and I know that he's as real as anything you might see on TV news. I've also learned the hard way that, when he does turn up, it's a good idea to listen very carefully to anything he might have to say.

Over the years I've come to realize that we all have a Mike inside us. Your Mike might be female rather than male, he might be old or he might be young—in some cases, I've heard, he can even turn up as an animal—but not many of us get to see him and talk to him as clearly and easily as Floyd did. Often, it's frustratingly hard to hear what he has to say. But in the hinge moments of our lives, those times when we stand at the dividing of the road and are not sure which route to take, he is the one who can unerringly point to the right path. He knows which way to go.

I don't know how he knows, but I've learned that you can trust that he is right and that the path he points to

promises wealth and riches in full and overflowing mea-
sure. It may not be the treasure you expected, or that you
thought you wanted at the start but when you find it, you
will discover it was exactly what your heart desired right
from the very beginning.

I sometimes think that learning to listen to him is one of
the main reasons we are here.

So, here's to you, Mike.

And thank you.

South Lake Tahoe